Death Trick

Also by Roderic Jeffries:

RODERIC JEFFRIES

Death Trick

An Inspector Alvarez novel

St. Martin's Press

New York

Library of Congress Cataloging-in-Publication Data

Jeffries, Roderic.
    Death trick / Roderic Jeffries.
        p. cm.
    ISBN 0-312-02189-5
    I. Title.
  PR6060.E43D45 1988
  823′.914—dc19   88-11589
                                             CIP

First published in Great Britain by William Collins Sons & Co., Ltd.
First U.S. Edition

10 9 8 7 6 5 4 3 2 1

Death Trick

CHAPTER 1

Pablo Roig studied with Pepysian pleasure the final figure on the sheet of paper—his capital wealth had increased yet again; not bad for a man who'd been born in a miserable casita and who'd once been a schoolmaster in a village school, obliged to speak deferentially to the mayor, the council, and any of the larger landowners who'd condescended to speak to him.

His rise from such humble beginnings had called for intelligence, ambition, hard work and a touch of genius. Intelligence had persuaded him to show respect to those he despised but who had the power to affect his future; ambition had been the spur which had driven him first to becoming a schoolmaster, then to qualifying as a solicitor; hard work had been the cement of his success; and the touch of genius had been to foresee what use could be made of the fact that Elena's cousin, Rodolfo, was a weakling. No one had liked Rodolfo, but as his father had been rich in land, no one had openly insulted him; yet only he, Pablo Roig, had seen reason to seek his company and buy him drink after drink while patiently listening to his stupid, rambling conversation ... Once satisfied that Rodolfo had reached a state of alcoholism which must ensure an early death, he'd proposed to Elena. Even though financially he was apparently a poor catch for any woman, he'd never doubted she'd accept him. After all, she'd already passed thirty—most women were married by twenty—and the best anyone could say about her looks was that she was kind-hearted. When people had heard of the engagement, they'd laughed; the laughs had been on the other sides of their faces when, eighteen months later and after Rodolfo's death, Rodolfo's father had died and left all his land to Elena.

If, he thought with continuing satisfaction, he were asked to define the art of success in business in one word, he'd say forethought. The ability to look ahead while the next man's eyes were fixed on the ground; to realize that the trickle of tourists must become a flood and developers would want to build near to the sea and that therefore a clever man did not sell land as soon as its value began to rise—as would the greedy peasant—but would hold on to it until the price had reached astronomical heights; to realize that foreigners who bought property would need legal assistance and that they would always patronize a solicitor who spoke their own languages, so that the hours spent learning English, French, and German, would eventually repay for themselves a thousand times over.

He mentally listed his major possessions, ignoring those which Elena had, in her stupid stubbornness, insisted on keeping in her own name. (On the Peninsula, the law had been far more sensible and just, holding that everything belonged to the husband.) The large estate among the foothills of the Sierra de Alfabia—about which she knew nothing, any more than about the many ladies who had visited him there; the fine properties, about which she did know, that he'd bought when clients had run into financial problems and needed money quickly (amusing to recollect that in at least two instances those financial problems had arisen because of his legal advice); the large portfolios of shares, held in Switzerland, about which the tax inspector knew nothing; the jewellery he'd given her because it was a fine investment rather than, as she thought, a token of his love and affection . . .

The intercom buzzed to interrupt his pleasant thoughts. He leaned forward and pressed down the switch.

'Señor Braddon is here with his wife and he says he must talk to you,' said Marta, his secretary.

'I'm too busy.'

'I told him you weren't seeing anyone, but he's insistent.'

'Tell him that I'm even more insistent that I'm too busy.' He once more leaned back in the chair. Marta was eighteen and very attractive, she responded to his verbal pleasantries with knowing pertness, and when his hand brushed her body she moved away casually rather than indignantly. But she had a novio. Could she be leading him on for as long as she judged it safe, because she was saving for married life? . . .

The intercom buzzed again.

'The señor says that you've got to see them.'

A wise man knew when to accept the inevitable. 'All right. Show them in in a couple of minutes.'

He picked up the sheet of paper and put it in the central drawer of the desk, which he locked. Although the figures could not possibly have meant anything to anyone else, life had taught him that a man could never be too secretive.

He prepared to smile a welcome to Braddon, a pompous fool who'd lived on the island for years and yet had not learned a word of Spanish, believing it to the the natives' duty to know English.

Marta showed the Braddons in. Roig stood, came round the desk, and shook hands. 'Señor Braddon; Señora Braddon, how nice to meet you again.' His English was fluent, his accent good. 'How well you both look.'

'I don't feel bloody well,' said Braddon resentfully, annoyed that he'd been unable to withdraw his hand in time to prevent its being seized with Continental exuberance.

'You have a cold, perhaps?'

'I have had a letter from you. Goddamn it . . .'

'Joe,' said Letitia warningly. She was thin and rather faded, as if she had been left in the sun too long.

'I told you, I'm not beating about the bush . . .'

'But it's much better if you stay calm.'

'And just how am I supposed to do that?'

'But it upsets your blood pressure so to get excited.'

'It's a wonder it's not gone through the bloody roof.'

Roig said soothingly: 'Let's all sit down and find out what has so upset the señor. I am certain we can very soon sort everything out. As one of our nineteenth-century philosophers said, There is a solution for everything, but death.'

'I don't give a . . .'

'Joe,' pleaded his wife.

They sat. The Braddons on chairs set in front of the desk. Roig smiled benignly at them. 'Now, tell me what is the trouble and I will help.'

'What d'you mean by your letter?' demanded Braddon.

'I did not explain myself clearly? I must apologize.' Roig thought that Braddon, with his beaky nose, and many chins, looked like an aged turkeycock.

'You explained yourself very clearly; don't make any mistake over that.'

'Then I am afraid I don't understand.'

'How the goddamn hell can you decide you won't represent me any longer?'

'But as I said in my letter, my wife is a cousin of the aparejador's wife and that is not a good relationship to have if one is going to court.'

'I like that! I really bloody like it! Not a good relationship to have!' His voice rose. 'Didn't you have it the day we first came here and talked about the trouble with the house?'

'But of course.'

'Why didn't you tell us about it then?'

'Because it was not necessary.'

'What d'you mean, not necessary? I've never heard anything bloody like it . . .'

'Please, Joe,' said Letitia, 'do keep calm.'

He swung round and seemed to be about to say something to her, but checked the words. After a moment, he turned back and spoke to Roig in a quieter manner. 'When we first came in here and I told you that cracks were appearing in some of the walls of the house, did you tell me I'd the right to sue the architect, the builder, and whatever the other man's called, because the house was less than ten years old?'

'That is exactly true.'

'And I handed you all the papers and plans which gave the names of the people concerned?'

'You did.'

'Then you could see right then that your cousin was involved?'

'It's my wife's cousin who is married to the aparejador, señor.'

'What's the difference? You could see it then? You knew right from the beginning there was a conflict of interests?'

'Indeed, no.'

'What the hell d'you mean? If you knew you're related to someone on the other side . . .'

'Señor, it is not I, but my wife who is . . .'

'The relationship meant there was a conflict of interests.'

'Not at that time.'

'What's that?' Braddon's growing anger was momentarily overtaken by surprise.

'Until a case actually goes to court, nothing can be so certain. Imagine what could happen here. I might die, my wife's cousin might die, far more regrettably, you might die. A hundred possibilities. So until it is known precisely what is to happen, how can one be certain there is a conflict of interests?'

Braddon's anger, reinforced, returned. 'In England, a solicitor with an ounce of honesty would have declared it immediately.'

'But, señor, here you are in Spain.'

'I don't bloody need reminding of that . . . Don't you make the mistake of thinking you're pulling the wool over my eyes. I now know exactly what's been going on. You're just a . . .'

'Please, Joe,' said Letitia.

He ignored her. 'You're just a miserable little crook.'

'That is not very polite,' said Roig sadly.

'I'm not trying to be polite. I'll say it again. You're a miserable little crook. You decided to keep your cousin out of trouble . . .'

'It is my wife's cousin who is the wife . . .'

Braddon expressed himself in terms which made Letitia wince, then continued: 'From the beginning, you've done all you could to string me along. You never told me that the court case had to be actually started within the ten years; you said that just writing to the other side was good enough. I couldn't understand what the hell was going on so I showed your letter to a friend this morning and he said that if I didn't start things actually rolling inside the ten-year period, I wouldn't have an action and now there are only days left. You've tried your damnedest to make certain I can't sue the bastards. But you won't get away with this. I'll speak to the College of Solicitors and tell 'em precisely what's happened; I'll see you're struck off the Rolls.'

Although his expression remained the same—suggesting concern that Braddon should be under such an unjustified misapprehension—Roig was amused. Did this pompous little man really believe that any complaint of his would carry weight? If every foreigner's complaint against his solicitor was acted upon, who'd be left to carry out the necessary legal work?

CHAPTER 2

Casa Gran, as was suggested by the name, was the largest home for many kilometres and it was set in grounds of a hundred and fifty hectares; any local farm of three hectares was considered to be of a good size. For over two centuries the estate had been owned by a Barcelona family but, despite their great wealth, they had supported the Republicans in the Civil War and all their property had, sooner or later, depending on the tides of battle, been confiscated. The island having declared for the Nationalists, the house was used as a barracks and inevitably had suffered considerable damage; after the war, it had been abandoned.

The two-room casita in which Roig had been born lay six kilometres to the south and on a clear day it had been possible to see Casa Gran from there; he could clearly remember, when young, standing in front of his mean, crude home and looking across the land. In identifying the big house for what it represented, he experienced the first surge of ambition that was to drive him forward and upward through life. At that time, however, such ambition had not reached so high as to envisage actual ownership of Casa Gran; that had come years later.

Eventually, the estate had come up for sale and he'd bought it. He'd spent a fortune on restoring the house to its former glory, satisfied that no one could mistake its new owner for anyone but a man of position and power. Often he would stand outside and look south and with deep satisfaction would once more reassure himself that it was impossible, even with the aid of glasses, to pick out the casita in which he'd once lived.

It always amused him that Elena had no idea he owned Casa Gran or to what use he put it. She was a woman of limited knowledge and even more limited curiosity. She had only three interests in life—her two children, traditional island crochet, and soap operas on television.

He parked the Citroën BX 19GT in front of Casa Gran and climbed out into the harsh sunlight, to stare up at the three-storey, stone-built house. Twenty-seven rooms. How many other men owned houses with twenty-seven rooms?

The entrance was traditional to the period, but unusual by modern standards; instead of a main doorway, there was an arched passageway which gave direct access to the inner courtyard, or patio, and off this there was on either side a tall, heavy wooden door, each of which led into an entrance hall. The courtyard was enclosed and so part of it was always in shade. In the centre was a fountain with a three-foot-high jet of recirculated water which dampened and freshened the air; radiating out, like the spokes of a wheel, were beds in which grew citrus trees and flowering bushes.

He entered the house through the right-hand doorway. 'Julia.' There was no answer. He called again. This time he heard her noisy approach as heels rapped on a flagstone floor.

She'd spent most of her working life in the fields and her long, narrow face was heavily lined, her skin dry and rough; she looked years older than he, yet was the younger by two months.

'Didn't you hear me call the first time?' he asked curtly.

'I was in the far room, cleaning,' she answered, in a flat, expressionless voice.

'A friend will be here soon; make certain everything's ready.' He wondered what were her thoughts concerning the women who visited him; but then perhaps she didn't really think about anything much? When they'd been young, they'd often played together if able to snatch time from working in the fields. Then, her family had owned the land they worked, whereas his had been sharecroppers. That had made her socially superior to him. He hoped she remembered those days so that she could fully appreciate the irony of the present ones. 'You can bring up a bottle of white wine and put it outside for me now.'

He went up the wide, curving staircase, with intricate wrought-iron banisters, to the landing, where he turned down the right-hand passage. The large, high-ceilinged bedroom was delightfully cool, even though the temperature outside was nearly 40°C. All the antique furniture glowed from recent polishing and the ancient floor tiles had been newly scrubbed; she might be little more intelligent than a cow, but she knew how to keep a house.

He changed out of his lightweight suit. In the summer,

few Mallorquins wore coats, let alone suits, but he had been told years ago by an Englishman that one could always distinguish an educated gentleman not by the way he behaved—a gentleman laid down his own standards of conduct—but by the way he dressed. He had never forgotten that. He put on a newly laundered cotton shirt and linen trousers, looked at his reflection in the full-length mirror on the door of the huge wardrobe; smart and trim, he decided with complacent pride.

He returned downstairs and went out into the courtyard. A table and two chairs had been set out on the shady side, near a tangerine tree on which the fruit was now the size of peas. He sat and poured himself a glass of wine. The grapes had been grown on his land and had been pressed in his press, the wine had matured in his cellars. A man of much property. He looked at his Breguet—Raquel would soon arrive. She hadn't been to Casa Gran before, so she was in for a big surprise; a surprise that would assuredly bring to an end her conquettish hesitations. He knew the growing excitement of expectation; as Julio Benavides had written, novelty was the sharpest of aphrodisiacs. The reverse was equally true. Eulalia should have remembered that. She'd really believed he'd divorce his wife to marry her. As if he could ever be such a fool as to lose all chance of gaining possession of the properties his wife retained in her own name with all the fervour of a miser! He remembered Eulalia the last time he'd seen her, made ugly by the tears streaming down her cheeks as she tried to remind him of all the promises he'd made when intent on seducing her. Was she really as naïve as she behaved?

It was comforting to be certain that Raquel would never subject him to such ridiculously emotional scenes. She knew the score. But as sophisticated as she might believe herself, he'd soon identified her weakness. She yearned to lead the kind of luxurious life which trashy reading and viewing had persuaded her the wealthy lived. So it hadn't taken many

dinners at the most expensive restaurants in Palma, or visits
to the Casino, to stop her pointing out the difference in their
ages . . .

He heard the crackling sounds of an approaching
motorized bike of some sort and he vaguely wondered who
this could be? Someone to speak to Julia, perhaps, but
certainly not Raquel; Raquel would never use so plebeian a
machine . . .

Julia came into the courtyard. 'There's a man who wants
to speak to you.'

'Who is he?' he asked irritatedly.

She shrugged her shoulders.

'Why the devil didn't you ask?'

She made no answer.

'Find out who he is and what he wants.' She really was
stupid, but if he sacked her that would be to forgo the
pleasure of employing her.

She returned. 'It's Carlos Vidal.'

'Never heard of him.'

'He says he wants to talk to you.'

'Is he a local?'

'He's a forastero,' she replied, using a term which signified
that he was a foreigner, not in the sense that he was not a
Spaniard, but that he did not come from the island.

'He can make an appointment to see me in the office.'

She left.

He watched a humming-bird hawk-moth hover in front
of a lantana in flower as he planned the course of the
seduction. One glass of wine and then he'd suggest a tour
of the house. She'd wonder if that was really wise, but finally
would agree. And in the master bedroom, he'd placed a
small piece of jewellery on the dressing-table . . .

'Señor.'

Startled, he looked round. Framed in the archway stood
a young man in faded shirt and patched jeans. 'What d'you
want?' he demanded roughly.

'The great favour of a word with you, señor.'

Andaluce, he judged immediately because of the way in which some of the words were slurred; a judgement confirmed by the jet-black hair, hawkish features, dark complexion, and last but not least, by his manner, which was one of insolent equality despite the poverty of his dress. 'Didn't you get my message?'

'The señora very kindly told me I should make an appointment at your office. But, señor, what I have to say is not for an office.'

'Then clear off.'

'You have been a friend of Señorita Eulalia Garcia, have you not?'

'That's none of your damned business.'

'She needs help. I am here to tell you that you must give it.'

For a moment, he was too surprised to speak; then the words came in a rush. 'Must! I must! A tattered gipsy comes here and tries to tell me what I must do!'

'Señor, she is very distressed . . .'

Roig shouted: 'Julia!'

She appeared so quickly that it was clear she had been close by, listening to what was said.

'Show him out.'

She spoke to Vidal in a low voice. He shook his head. She spoke again, with more urgency, gesticulating with her hands. He shook his head a second time. She shrugged her shoulders and was silent.

'Señor, I beg of you to understand . . .' began Vidal.

'Tell Pedro to come here and throw this bloody man out,' Roig shouted.

'Señor, you are making a very serious mistake.'

'I'll tell you something, it's you who's making the bad mistake; as you'll find out soon enough when Pedro gets here.'

'I have tried to speak with you, señor.' Vidal's manner

remained courteous. 'It is not my fault that you are too stupid to listen.' He bowed briefly, turned, and left; his back was proudly straight, as if he had just been awarded two ears and a tail.

CHAPTER 3

Roig turned off the main Llueso/Puerto Llueso road on to a dirt track and the Citroën lurched into and out of potholes, despite its forgiving suspension. Just as well, he thought, that he wasn't in the Porsche 928 which he'd so nearly bought from a German who'd run into financial troubles in his business because of bad legal advice. As beautifully made as they were, they weren't for this kind of chassis-wrecking surface. Yet what a temptation it had been! The smart and the rich had been running Porsches for a couple of years, ever since it had become easier and cheaper to own a foreign made car . . . Yet he was a clever man who could recognize that there were times when it was wiser not to appear too smart or too rich. Now was such a time. In recent years, the system of taxation had changed from a levy on a group (with members of that group deciding what proportion of the total demanded each of them should bear) to individual assessment. Originally, every Mallorquin had laughed at this fresh stupidity from Madrid. But slowly it was becoming painfully clear that one really was going to have to provide figures which would be accepted by a beady-eyed, suspicious, vindictive, forastero tax inspector, or suffer very severe consequences. And if one were running a Porsche 928, how did one convince that man that one had virtually no capital and earned no more than a million?

He slowed as he came abreast of an ugly house. Almost there. And to his angry annoyance, he recognized that he was very reluctant to meet Oakley. Why? What had he to fear? He was just as clever, as he'd proved over the past few months. Or had he? Had Oakley somehow discovered the truth? Impossible. Yet, if Oakley had, then that hint of steel beneath the cheerful, friendly, ironic exterior, might come more sharply into focus . . .

He turned into a narrower and rougher track—almond trees to the right, orange and lemon trees to the left—and continued to the end where there was a turning circle, in the centre of which was an olive with gnarled, hollow trunk and a fan of branches which spoke of regular pruning. Beyond was an old stone farmhouse.

As he stepped out of the car, Oakley came through the doorway of the house. ''Morning. Very kind of you to come along.'

Since it had been more of an order than a request, the words could have been ironic; yet Oakley's expression suggested only friendly gratitude. Roig never trusted people who could conceal their thoughts. 'I had business at this end of the island in any case, señor.'

'Good. Then I haven't upset your working day . . . But do forget the señor. As I've told you before, I'm Gerald or Gerry; provided, of course, that it's spelt with a G.' He smiled.

Roig couldn't understand the significance of that and had the uncomfortable feeling he was being mocked.

'But let's move, out of the sun. It really has been too hot these past few days, even for me. Yet according to the BBC this morning, in London it's overcast and cool. If only we could swap a little of our sun for a little—and only a little —of their cool.'

The farmhouse was typical of its period, built long before foreigners had come to live on the island and basically owing everything to need and nothing to aesthetics; the walls were of stone, bonded by Mallorquin cement which powdered, the shallow roof was supported by timber beams, the windows were small and originally had had solid wooden shutters which had done away with the need for glass. In the past few years it had been reformed and the work had obviously been done under the supervision of someone with taste and intelligence.

They passed through two rooms, the one leading directly into the other, and out on to the south-facing patio. Overhead vines, trained over wires, provided a shade which shimmered as the very light breeze stroked the leaves.

'Grab a seat,' said Oakley, 'and tell me what you'd like to drink?'

'A whisky, please.'

As Oakley returned into the house, Roig sat and looked out. Beyond the patio was a small garden bounded by a low drystone wall and then a field, recently harvested, in which grew fig, almond, and algaroba trees; several sheep were grazing the stubble. As a boy, living in the casita, one of his jobs had been to herd their small flock of sheep. These had had such little grazing, of such poor quality, that they'd forever been breaking out in search of something more to eat. Each time they'd escaped him, his father had beaten him with a thick leather strap. He hated sheep, couldn't even enjoy eating lamb, although one might have thought that that would furnish a welcome revenge . . .

Oakley returned. 'One Scotch.' He put a glass down in front of Roig, sat, raised his own glass. 'Health, wealth, and happiness; and I leave you to place them in order of priority.'

Was that a malicious dig at his values? Roig didn't know the answer and silently cursed his inability to understand Oakley.

'I thought it would be an idea to have a chat—quite apart from the pleasure of meeting again.'

Roig drank.

'Things aren't going too well, are they?'

'Aren't they?' Roig said, trying to sound surprised.

'For one thing, the sales of plots of land haven't proved as high as projected . . .'

'I did say from the beginning that we were asking far too much per square metre.'

'Yes, that's right, you did, but I still disagree with you. The cutting edge of our sales pitch is that we're offering exclusivity; the world's become so democratic that one can't demand good breeding, so one has to rely on wealth and shut one's eyes to the accompanying vulgarity. We've made certain that only the rich will buy into the urbanización.'

Roig couldn't decide how serious Oakley was being.

'But, in fact, that's not really the issue; if it were merely a case of depressed sales, I wouldn't be worrying because I'm convinced that once a sufficient number of people complain loudly enough about the ridiculous prices we're charging, we'll sell everything . . . No, what really bothers me is that there seems to be a heavy drain on resources which isn't immediately explainable, but is putting us into serious trouble. D'you know anything about it?'

'Why should I?'

'Why? Because, Pablo, I have a very great respect for your intelligence.'

'I do not understand.'

'Don't try to hide behind your overdeveloped sense of modesty.'

Roig, again wondering whether Oakley was speaking seriously or mockingly, uncertain how much was known or guessed, experienced a growing fear. He drained his glass.

'You are beyond any doubt a very sharp and intelligent man. That, of course, is why I approached you to join the company in the first instance. That and the fact that you equally obviously are a man who—how shall I put this?— knows how to fix things greatly to his advantage.'

What did that really mean?

'So, because you're a clever man, Pablo, perhaps you've begun to suspect that someone could be swindling the company?'

'Certainly not. That's impossible,' he replied, with more emphasis than he'd intended.

'Impossible or improbable? Or would you say that the answer's far more likely to lie in thoughtless inefficiency rather than in thoughtful dishonesty? Frankly, I hope that that is not so. Thoughtful dishonesty can be sharply reversed, thoughtless inefficiency can take a fatal time to correct. And it's beginning to look as if we don't have much time in hand.' Oakley stood. 'You'll have a refill, won't you?' He did not immediately move away after picking up the glasses, but remained by the table. 'If you've reason to suspect there may be something going on but, being a lawyer, you only speak out when you're twice certain, have a word on the quiet with whoever's concerned and suggest that if all the ill-gotten gains are refunded . . .'

'I know nothing.'

'Then there's no need to continue and I can, as the Scots so aptly put it, save my breath for cooling the porridge. Though the thought of porridge in this temperature . . .' He smiled, left, and went into the house.

Roig thought about everything that had been said and his fear subsided and was replaced by a sense of comforting superiority. Clearly, Oakley had not the slightest idea of exactly what had been going on . . .

CHAPTER 4

Julia Monserrat awoke. The year before, she would have left the bed immediately, but she allowed herself a further few minutes' rest; it was one concession to a perpetually tired and aching body she now allowed.

From the other bedroom there came the sound of snoring. She'd heard Adolfo return, but had no idea what time of the night that had been. From the noise, he'd been

tight again. She sighed. She kept trying to persuade him
not to drink so much, but his job as a waiter in a café
militated against her efforts. It was a tragedy that his
father, who would surely have taught him more sense
than she'd been able to do, had died when he was only
five.

So many years without a man, she thought as she stared
up at the still darkened ceiling. Her friends often complained
that their husbands were forever demanding and told her
how lucky she was to be able to lead her own life; she never
replied that meeting a thousand demands was far preferable
to perpetual loneliness.

She switched on the light, climbed out of bed, and went
into the bathroom. There was running water now. That and
the electricity were the only changes there had been since
her husband had died. Even if she'd had the money for
extensive improvements—friends had altered their houses
almost beyond recognition—she wasn't certain she'd have
had the work done; somehow it seemed right to keep the
house as near as possible to how it had been when her
husband had been alive.

She went out and into the barn which was built on to the
side of the house. Here, she milked the only cow that was
lactating, then collected up an armful of fodder for the
rabbits. These were plagued by myxomatosis—she'd lost
two in the past week—and after feeding them she took down
the sacking over the fronts of the wooden cages and resoaked
this in disinfectant before replacing it. She began to carry
the pail of milk to the kitchen, but was reminded by the two
cats that they had not yet been given their small ration of
milk and she turned back to fill the shallow earthenware
bowl they used. That done, she took the milk through. When
she returned from work that afternoon, she must water the
tomatoes and pick beans ready for her friend to take to the
market the next day . . . Life would have been a lot easier
if only Adolfo had given a hand, but he flatly refused, saying

that he did his work at the café and when he was at home, he rested.

For breakfast, she ate a plateful of milk and bread. Then she bicycled the six kilometres to Casa Gran. Much of the journey was uphill and recently she'd been finding the effort of pedalling very much harder, but she'd no thought of giving up the job because she needed the money to keep the house going. When Adolfo had started work, she'd expected him to pay towards his keep. He never had.

She began to sweat, although normally she looked too dried-up to be capable of doing so. She waved to an old friend, at work in a field, and had hurriedly to grab the handlebars to keep her balance. Less than a year ago, through waving to someone else, she'd fallen and had cut and bruised her ankle so badly that she'd been unable to go to Casa Gran for several days. Roig had turned up at her house and had threatened to get someone else unless she returned immediately, long before the ankle had properly healed . . .

She thought she understood Roig's motive for humiliating and bullying her, but not the reasoning behind such motive. How could he sensibly blame her for the way life had been when they'd been young? And how could he now be so blind to decency as to flaunt his excesses in front of her? Not that one could really use the word 'decency' where his women were concerned. No better than cheap whores. Except for poor Eulalia. So innocent, she had been seduced by words of love. Roig would never commit a crime greater than speaking those words . . .

She turned on to the dirt track which led to the big house. Ferriol was spraying vines and when he saw her he stopped and came across, sliding the knapsack sprayer off his shoulders as he came up to where she waited. He nodded a good morning. She pointed at the nearest row of staked vines. 'They're looking all right.'

'There'll be a crop, if it don't rain heavy.' Much rain

between now and the harvest would create meteorological
history, but if one worked on the land, one did not tempt
fate by assuming favourable weather.

There was a long silence, which she broke. 'I'd better
move on and start some work.'

'Aye. He's up there.'

'The señor is?' Despite her contempt for the way he
behaved, she never referred to him without the respectful
title.

'He was there when I arrived; leastwise, his car was.'

'Then maybe he's spent the night here.'

'With the latest, like as not, so he won't have done much
sleeping.' He chuckled salaciously.

She showed her disapproval of such talk. Ferriol was far
too interested in the women up at the house—a man of his
age should have calmed down.

She climbed on to the bicycle and cycled up the track and
round to the back of the house, which faced the mountains.
Roig's Citroën was parked outside the garage; she was
vaguely surprised that if he had spent the night in the house,
he had not put the car under cover since he normally fussed
obsessively over all his possessions. She left her bike, crossed
the cobbled yard to a stone urn, and felt underneath this for
the key to the main back door which wouldn't be unlocked
because Roig never used it—the back door was for servants.
She unlocked the door and went in. The passage gave access
to the unfurnished room in which she kept all the cleaning
things. She lifted an apron from one of the hooks, picked up
the cane basket in which were dusters and furniture polish,
and left. Today was the day for polishing the furniture in
the bedrooms.

Although the house was large, its basic layout was simple
and there was a direct, if rather lengthy, route to the living
quarters. She entered the left-hand hall and was about to
cross to the stairs when she checked herself. From the room
now on her right there came a strange sound, rising and

falling both in tone and pitch, which she could not immediately identify, but which for some reason disturbed her. She hesitated, then crossed to the door and knocked—in a spirit of contempt, he had ordered her to knock before entering any room; in truth, she would never have done otherwise for fear of what disgusting scene she might witness if she did not. There was no answer to her knock and the sound inside continued. She opened the door. The body of Roig was slumped across one of the tapestry chairs and it had become an attraction for a swarm of blowflies. She crossed herself.

CHAPTER 5

Alvarez stared down at the untidy pile of papers on his desk, an expression of sad bewilderment on his pudgy face. Ten years ago, perhaps even as little as five, that quantity of paperwork would have encompassed a couple of months' crime, yet now it barely represented a fortnight's. Where would it all end?

He slumped back in the chair. Politicians. They created the troubles of the world, but left others to clear up the mess, vilifying them when the task proved impossible. Anyone but a politician would have known that to relax the laws against drugs was an act of insanity. Yet the present government had done just that and so now one could buy any drug one fancied in Puerto Llueso—if one wasn't mugged first. Puerto Llueso, so beautiful, it clutched at a man's soul, once so peaceful it had seemed as if angels often gathered there . . .

The telephone rang. His caller was the superior chief's plum-voiced secretary who said that Señor Salas wished to speak to him. As he waited, he modified his previous conclusion. The problems of the world were created by politicians and superior chiefs.

'Alvarez—presumably you've heard about the murder in Prevaix?'

'I read an account in the paper, señor, but . . .'

'In his practice, Roig dealt with a large number of foreigners. The investigating inspector, Jaume, speaks no foreign languages which makes for difficulties, so you are to assist him.'

'But surely he can . . .'

'Why do you always have to argue? It is an unfortunate fact that you are the only inspector on the island with an adequate knowledge of any foreign language; were there any other even partially competent linguist available, rest assured I would never call on you to help, since bitter experience has shown that you delight in complicating the simplest of issues. Why I, who have always done my duty and honoured State and Church, should have to bear such a crippling cross, I just do not understand.' He cut the connection.

Alvarez checked the time. Ten to one. Even if Jaume was still in his office, he'd be on the point of leaving it to go home to lunch; if he was not in his office, there was small point in phoning. The call could reasonably be left until after lunch.

Rising a little late from his siesta, Alvarez did not return to the guardia post until well after five. He climbed the stairs, sweating from the exertion, and went along to his room, where he slumped down in the chair to recover his breath. He looked at the telephone with a sense of bitterness and cursed Jaume—a man whom he normally liked. Why the devil couldn't Jaume cope with his own problems, instead of incompetently forcing them on to others? As Alvarez slowly regained his breath, his mood became less belligerent. Jaume was smart, so surely there was every chance that by now he'd found out who'd murdered Roig and there'd be nothing to do . . .

'You must be joking!' said Jaume, the telephone exaggerating his gravelly voice which ill-suited his small, slim build.

Alvarez's gloom returned.

'It's not too much of an exaggeration to say that right now all we know for certain is that he's dead.'

'No obvious suspects?'

'He was enough of a bastard that I reckon anyone who knew him could be called a suspect . . . But as a matter of fact, there was a caller at the house in the late afternoon and there was a row between him and Roig.'

'Then surely there's every chance that that's who you're looking for?'

'But all we know about him is that he spoke English and drove a white Seat 127. How many white 127s d'you think there are on the island?'

'God knows.'

'Perhaps. But I wouldn't bet on it. And in any case, we've nothing to say that he was still around at the earliest estimated time of death, which is ten.'

'What about the murder knife?'

'It came from the kitchen—the daily identifies it.'

'Were there any dabs on it?'

'Quite a few, but an initial check shows they were all the daily's.'

'Doesn't that make her a suspect?'

'That life should be so easy! She left the house at around five and that's confirmed by the farm labourer who saw her cycling off. She went straight home and cooked a meal for herself and her son and then went on to a neighbour's place to help nurse the sick wife. There are three people to swear she was in that house from around eight to well after one the next morning.'

'Has she any idea who the murderer might be?'

'None that helps us, since she inclines to the idea that

Roig's death was inspired by the Almighty as a punishment for his wicked life.'

'Was it wicked?'

'Depends on your definitions; mine say he had a whale of a time. Seems like there was a succession of women, much younger than himself, and enthusiastic. But the daily's one of the old brigade who reckons life should be dull; became almost incoherent at one point, saying he'd ruined sweet innocence and deserved to die. I'll bet they were innocent!'

'Have you talked to any of 'em?'

'I've only been able to identify the last one and there's not been the time to get hold of her yet.'

'Did his wife know what was going on?'

'Frankly, although she's obviously not prostrated with grief, I've thought it best to keep off the subject for a bit. Still, if you ask me to guess, I'd say she had a pretty shrewd idea. All the daily can say is that she's never seen the wife at Casa Gran. Obviously, that was Roig's secret love-nest.'

'The rich lead different lives, don't they?'

'Envy won't get you anywhere.'

'Can the daily give a good description of the man in the 127?'

'She was upstairs when the car arrived and she looked out of the window, but saw only the top of his head; ordinary brown hair, straight, perhaps beginning to bald at the crown. When she went downstairs, the two men were in the main sitting-room and she'd no cause to go in there. Just before leaving, she heard Roig shouting, but it was in English so she's no idea what he was saying; the visitor was talking in a normal voice and as the door is very solid, all she caught was a murmur.'

'Not very promising.'

'I told you, so far it's a real cow. But on top of that, I'm feeling like death.'

'Sorry to hear that.'

'Look, Enrique, there's something you can do for me right

away. There were a few papers about the place and we came across one with a note of a telephone number—530782. That's your end of the island, so check it through and find out if it can have any significance, will you? I need to get hold of something that'll keep Salas quiet.'

'Try strychnine.'

Jaume chuckled.

When the call was over, Alvarez looked through the drawers of the desk for a copy of the telephone directory, eventually found that he'd used it to prop up the corner of a very battered cupboard. Because numbers were listed under separate towns and villages, it did not take him long to discover that the one Jaume had given him belonged to Gerald Oakley of Ca'n Tardich, Carretera Llueso/Puerto Llueso, s/n. Oakley sounded to be an English name; Roig had spoken English to the visitor to Casa Gran on Monday morning.

Twenty minutes later, he drove up the narrow dirt track and parked in the shade of the olive tree which stood outside Ca'n Tardich. He climbed out of the car. In his fantasies, this was the kind of house he'd buy after winning the lottery . . .

He rang the bell to the right of the front door and then, when there was no answer, walked round to the vine-covered patio. He stared at the sheep in the field, their neck-bells clanking as they moved, and he thought how, if the land were his, he'd drill for water and when successful would turn the parched field into a cornucopia of beans, peas, peppers, aubergines, tomatoes, onions, garlic, radishes, strawberries, artichokes, lettuces . . .

He returned to the car and drove off, stopping outside the ugly, square house that stood on the wider dirt track. Two young girls were playing with dolls on a patch of weed grass and he asked them if their mother was around; the elder ran into the house. When she returned, she was accompanied by a woman who held a baby in her arms.

'I'm sorry to disturb you, señora.'

'It's nothing,' she answered, with the weary acceptance of someone whose every waking hour, and many of her sleeping ones, were disturbed.

'I'm looking for Señor Oakley.'

'He lives over there.' She pointed in the direction of Ca'n Tardich.

'I've just been there, but the house is locked. I wondered if you'd any idea where he might be?'

She shook her head. 'We don't really say anything but good-morning to each other.'

'Have you seen him today?'

She thought. 'I've not seen him for a day or two, but then I've been tied up with the baby who's teething . . .' As if to underline her words, the baby began to cry loudly; she rocked him in her arms.

He scratched his chin and his fingers rasped across stubble, reminding him that he'd forgotten to shave that morning. 'D'you know anyone who might be able to tell me where I could find him?'

'There's Beatriz—she looks after the house.'

'Where does she live?'

'In the village, in Calle General Ayer, but I don't know the number.'

'I'll soon find that out. Thanks, señora, and I hope the baby's teeth will soon calm down.'

'You can't hope that any more than I do!'

He drove on to the main road and then round to the west side of Llueso, often referred to as the new part although the houses were, on average, well over fifty years old. At the start of Calle General Ayer, a boy on a skateboard—the craze had not yet entirely disappeared—said that Beatriz, who worked for foreigners, lived at No. 21. He continued on to a house half way along the street on the left-hand side. Like all the others, it appeared drab from the outside despite the brightly painted shutters and window-boxes filled with flowers; but inside it was considerably more spacious than might have been expected and was spotlessly clean; beyond the second downstairs room there was visible a small patio in which grew an orange tree.

Beatriz was in her middle forties, small of body, but clearly sharp of mind, and never still; she reminded him of a sparrow at nesting time. 'Why d'you want to know about the señor?'

He explained.

'Then . . .' She stopped.

'Then what, señora?'

'Then something really has happened to him.'

'Why d'you say that?'

She did not answer him directly. 'I wondered whether I ought to tell someone. Then I thought that maybe that was being stupid. I mean, a man doesn't always act the same as ever, does he?'

'Has he been acting strangely?'

She gestured with her hands. 'He's never before gone off without telling me. And the señora came to see what was wrong because he'd been meant to have a meal with her but never turned up.'

'Suppose you tell me what's been happening?'

She nodded, but went into the next room to return with some knitting; she knitted quickly as she spoke. She worked for Oakley and two other persons down in the port. She went to Ca'n Tardich in the mornings on Mondays, Wednesdays, and Fridays. It wasn't the señor's house, but he rented it from another Englishman who had obtained it on a life lease—which included a clause permitting sub-letting—and had reformed it. He'd first lived there about . . . Must be two years back. He wasn't there all the time; just came and went, never staying very long.

He always told her when he was going away and wrote or telephoned to say when he was returning. Yet last Wednesday she had arrived at the house and although he'd not been there, the house had been unlocked. At first, she'd thought nothing of that. He'd gone out shopping or visiting and had forgotten to lock up—not that he'd ever done so before. But he didn't turn up by the time she left and that was even more unusual, because she was due to be paid and he'd never before forgotten to pay her; if he was not going to be in when she finished, he left the money in the kitchen —but there'd been no money there. Perhaps, for some reason, he'd left it somewhere else? She'd checked the three rooms she hadn't cleaned that morning; no money. But in the spare bedroom, one of the paintings had been swung back, revealing the wall safe it normally concealed; the door was open and the safe was empty. It did seem very strange he should have left it like that . . .

She'd locked up the house. By now definitely uneasy, she'd looked in the garage; the car wasn't there. This seemed to confirm that he'd left, in a tearing hurry . . . As she'd been about to leave, a car had driven up and the driver had leaned through the open window and called her over. The señora hadn't had the manners even to say good-morning, but had spoken very rapidly in English and had become annoyed when asked to speak more slowly. It appeared that the señor had been invited to a meal at her house the previous night, had accepted, but had never turned up. The señora had three times telephoned to find out what was the matter, but there'd been no answer. So now she wanted to speak to him . . .

'I don't think she was worried about the possibility the señor could be ill,' said Beatriz. 'She was just furious because he hadn't turned up at her place.'

'D'you know who she is?'

'Her name's Señora Neatherley; she and the señor have been to Señor Oakley's more than once. Her husband's a much more pleasant person.'

'Where do they live?'

'Up in the urbanización, but I've no idea which house.'

'You're being very helpful. There's something else you can maybe tell me. Has a man called Señor Roig ever visited the señor's house?'

'I'm certain he hasn't,' she answered confidently. But then she added: 'But I do seem to know the name.'

'Could it be that he's telephoned some time and you've taken the call?'

'D'you know, I think that's right. In fact, now I remember exactly. It's not all that long ago when the telephone rang and the señor was out, so I answered. The caller wanted the señor to ring him back as soon as possible; he said his name was Señor Roig.'

'I wish everyone had as good a memory as you . . . A bit earlier on, you spoke of the señor's car—what kind is it?'

'A Seat 127.'

'And the colour?'

'White.'

'One last thing. What would you say the top of the señor's head looks like?'

'What's that?'

He smiled. 'I haven't gone round the bend! What colour's his hair?'

'Just an ordinary brown.'

'Straight?'

'That's right.'

'Beginning to show signs of baldness?'

'He quite often jokes and says that he'll be completely bald in a couple of years and then he'll be a very old man. As I always tell him, there's a good bit of life left in him yet.'

'You sound as if you like him?'

'I've worked for enough foreigners to know they come in all sorts—he's the best. Doesn't think we're stupid just because we do things in a different way. And he'll sit down with me for a cup of coffee in the middle of the morning;

you'd be surprised how many of 'em would sooner be dead
than be seen doing that.'

'I don't think I would.' He stood.

She stared up at him. 'You think something has happened
to him?'

'I simply don't know at the moment.' He thanked her,
said goodbye, and left. He was not surprised that the name
of Roig had evoked no startled reaction. News of the murder
had been in all the papers, but few women bothered to read
about events which took place beyond their own villages
and it had not been mentioned on the television.

CHAPTER 6

Alvarez reluctantly climbed out of bed, to sit on the edge.
He stared at the closed shutters, the slats and the sun
creating bars of harsh light, and yawned.

'Come on,' Dolores shouted from downstairs.

He wondered how she managed to be so bright and sharp
this early; too sharp, if the truth were told . . .

'Enrique, it's after eight.'

He stood, padded across to the window, unclipped the
shutters and pushed them open and back against the wall.
The heat surged in. He stared across the roof-tops at the
sugarloaf-shaped Puig Antonia, on top of which was the
untidy huddle of buildings of Santa Antonia, once a hermi-
tage, now occupied by nuns. They had almost certainly
been up and about for hours. Maybe there was something
about a holy life that made it easier to get up in the morning?

Ten minutes later, he went downstairs. Dolores, his
cousin—the relationship was, in fact, more remote than
that—was already preparing lunch and she looked up from
the vegetables she was peeling. 'You're getting up later
every morning.'

'That's because I'm becoming older every morning.'

'Then you need less sleep.'

He sat at the table. It was no good arguing with her. A fine, handsome woman, a wife to be trusted in all circumstances, but far too fond of having the last word. Jaime should have dealt with that trait at the beginning of their marriage, but he was essentially a lazy man who preferred a peaceful life to one of challenge . . .

'Has the good Lord seized your wits during the night?'

He started. 'What's that?'

'Since you sat down, you've done nothing but stare into space. Why? Is the coca no good?'

'It's fine,' he reassured her hastily, well aware of how annoyed she became if ever she thought her cooking was being criticized. He crumbled the end of the slice of sponge-like coca into the cocoa, ate. 'What's for lunch?'

'We're starting with Sopas Mallorquin.'

'There's no one on the island can make a sopas to touch yours.'

She nodded. 'And then there'll be pork chops.'

'With alioli?'

'But of course.' She spoke with surprise. Would any cook serve pork chops without garlic sauce?

Fifteen minutes later, he was in his office. He called Traffic on the telephone and asked them to find out the number of Oakley's car. Half an hour after that, they rang back to say that the number was PM 12050.

He slumped back in the chair. Assume for the moment that Oakley's disappearance betokened flight, then surely he would not have taken his car since that could be so readily traced; but he would have needed to reach a jumping-off point . . . He sat upright, leaned forward and lifted the telephone receiver. He made three calls; the first was to the airport, asking the police to check all cars parked there (a request that was met with an angry demand to know whether he realized how much work was involved); the second was to the docks, with a similar request; the third was to Traffic, asking them to put out a general call for information on the white Seat.

As he replaced the receiver, he yawned. He looked at his watch—merienda-time. He went downstairs and out to the street and then walked along up to the old square. Tourists were drinking at the many tables, in the shade of trees, set out in front of the cafés which fronted the square. Life was fun for those who didn't have to work, he thought. He went into the bar in the Club Llueso, ordered a coffee and a brandy, and sat.

The Neatherleys' house was almost at the top of the urbanización. Because of the shape of the hill, it had needed extensive foundations and the cost of building had been over a third more than it would have been on flatter land. From it there was a magnificent view across to Llueso Bay but, decided Alvarez, only a foreigner could ever have decided this worth the extra cost.

A maid, wearing an apron, showed him into a large sitting-room whose picture windows faced south and the bay. Constance Neatherley entered. She had a beaky face, overshot teeth, and a manner which flatly contradicted the proposition that all persons were equal. In the days of Empire, she could have been found anywhere from Ascension to Zanzibar instructing the natives on how to do things her way.

In summer, she wore cotton frocks whose cut and colours did not suit her and no make-up to hide the roughness of her skin. Her string of pearls were cultivated, but she always referred to them as natural, being a woman of refinement. She accepted it as her duty to set by example the standards to be maintained among the expatriate community (the British community, that was; she doubted that the smaller French, German, and American ones had standards).

She listened to what Alvarez said, noting with distaste his

crumpled shirt and creased trousers. 'And if I do know Mr Oakley, is that any concern of yours?'

'Señora, I wish to speak with him.'

'Why bother me with that fact?'

'Beatriz, his maid, says the señor was expected to have supper with you on Tuesday, but did not turn up.'

'Dinner,' she corrected.

'Perhaps you have heard from him since then?'

'I have not.' She spoke sharply. Nothing excused bad manners. She crossed to the nearer armchair and sat. She did not suggest that he did the same.

'Then you cannot tell me where he is now?'

'No.'

'But perhaps you could suggest the name of a friend of his who might be able to help me?'

'Just what is this all about?'

'As I said . . .'

'I am perfectly well aware of what you said. But that doesn't answer my present question.'

'I wish to speak with Señor Oakley.'

'About what?'

'I will explain that to him when I see him.'

She was annoyed by his insolent answer and was about to express herself on the subject when there was the sound of a car door being slammed. She turned and looked at the doorway. A man entered. 'Hullo, there,' he said jovially to Alvarez. 'Don't think we've met?'

'He's from the police.' Her tone was frigid.

'Is that so?' Neatherley was well-fleshed, largely because he ate and drank generously whenever he had the opportunity. Gregarious by nature, his wife had had to rescue him from several friendships which she, with her finer feelings, would have found very distasteful, had they been prolonged. 'The police, eh? What have you been up to, old girl?'

Her lips tightened. Since marrying him thirty-five years ago, she had succeeded in eliminating most of his more unwelcome traits, but she never had been able to cure him of his appalling sense of humour. 'Thomas!'

'All right. Just . . .'

'The Inspector is asking questions about Gerald.'

'Gerry? The old dog! So what has he . . .' He came to a mumbling stop as he saw the gathering expression on her face. He hurriedly said to Alvarez: 'I say, don't keep standing. Grab a seat. And what'll you drink?'

'It is far too early to start drinking,' she said crisply.

'But the people here don't bother about yardarms as we do . . .'

'Stop waffling.'

'Yes, dear.'

Alvarez sat and briefly pondered something he'd once read or been told. Upper-class Englishwomen overcame their refined distaste for the carnal desires of their husbands by visualizing Wordsworth's daffodils. He decided Señora Neatherley had chosen seldom to need to contemplate daffodils.

Neatherley stood in front of the fireplace, in which was set a wood-burning stove, and put his hands in the pockets of his immaculately laundered linen trousers. He cleared his throat. 'I hope Gerry's not in any sort of trouble?'

'At the moment, señor, my only brief is to find him so that I can speak to him.'

'Kind of disappeared, has he? As a matter of fact, we invited him over for an evening meal . . .'

'He knows about that,' she said.

'Oh! Really? Odd his not turning up; I mean, you'd expect him to get in touch if something had happened . . .'

She interrupted him again as she spoke to Alvarez. 'We have not seen him, or heard from him, since he accepted my invitation. There is, therefore, no way in which we can help you.'

'Not directly, señora, but perhaps indirectly you may be able to.'

She was annoyed; it was always difficult to deal with someone who lacked the social wit to realize when he was being politely told it was time to go.

'I would like to understand what kind of a man he is. You are his friends and so will be able to tell me that.'

'I do not know what you're talking about.'

'He means . . .' began Neatherley.

'Thomas!'

He rattled some coins in one of his pockets.

'Is he a happy man, señora, or does he have troubles?'

'We all have troubles.'

'But has he seemed worried about anything recently?'

'Perhaps I should make myself perfectly clear. Many people believe friendship is a reason for the exchange of endless intimacies; I do not.'

'But I feel certain you have been able to judge whether he has seemed to be worried about something?'

'Gerry's been as full of beans as ever,' said Neatherley. 'Never met a bloke who can so look on the bright side of things as he does.'

'Is he a clever man, señor?'

'I'd call him that, wouldn't you, Constance?'

'He has good manners, which is far more important. Or perhaps I should say, he appeared to have them until Tuesday.'

'Do you know where he lives when not on the island?'

'I have not the slightest idea.'

Neatherley said: 'He obviously moves around the Continent a good bit and also goes back to the UK.' His tone changed slightly. 'But now I come to think of it, I don't remember his ever mentioning what I'd call a definite home. D'you, Constance?'

'I have already answered that question.'

'But he must have one somewhere. He can't spend all his life living out of a suitcase, can he?'

She didn't bother to answer.

'If he travels a great deal, perhaps he is in some kind of business?' suggested Alvarez.

'I'm pretty sure he is,' said Neatherley. 'I remember I was chatting to him one day about development on this island and how it had gone wild and ruined the whole place and the people who were building now were bound to lose a lot of money and he said that there was still room for good profit if one knew what one was doing. There was something about the way he spoke which made me wonder if he could be in property development.'

'Can you remember what it was that made you think that?'

'Damned if I can now. Have you any idea, Constance?'

'No,' she answered wearily.

It seemed clear that he would learn nothing more. Alvarez stood. 'Thank you, señora, señor, for your help.'

She was surprised. It seemed he'd actually dredged up enough manners to leave.

The telephone rang and Alvarez leaned across the desk to pick up the receiver.

'Airport police here. That Seat you were asking about is in the car park, opposite Terminal A. There's a ticket on the dashboard which says it was left there just before midday on Tuesday.'

When the call was over, he rang Jaume's office, but was informed that the inspector was away ill. He asked the man at the other end of the line to pass on the information to whoever continued the investigation.

He replaced the receiver and knew a warm contentment. Jaume had been unable to request any further assistance, no fresh crime of any importance in Llueso had been reported, and the only letter to arrive that day could safely be ignored. He closed his eyes, the better to appreciate his blessings.

CHAPTER 7

Even over the telephone, Salas's resentment was obvious. 'Inspector Jaume is ill.'

'So I understand, señor,' said Alvarez.

'In view of the investigation into the murder of Roig, it is very unfortunate. It means someone else must take over the case immediately.'

'I've left a note of the results of my inquiries for whoever does . . .'

'You will.'

'I will what, señor?'

'Damnit, can't you understand the simplest order? You are to take charge of the investigations into the murder of Roig.'

'But . . .'

'In view of the fact that you are already conversant with some of the details and because foreigners are involved, I'm left with no alternative. If I had one, I'd take it.'

'But I have so much work in hand . . .'

'Keep me fully informed of every single development and on no account are you to take any direct action without reference to me. Is that clear?'

'Yes, señor, but . . .' The line had gone dead. Alvarez slowly replaced the receiver. Was it really only a short time ago that he'd been congratulating himself on his good fortune?

The eight-year-old Seat 127 was in the middle of the fifth row of covered parking bays. The uniform sargento produced a key and unlocked the passenger door, reached inside, and brought out a ticket. 'Here you are.'

Alvarez moved more fully into the shade of the corrugated

iron roof before he examined the ticket. It had been issued at eleven fifty-two on Tuesday; say, fourteen hours after the murder. Of course, this could be merely a coincidence. But if one remembered that Oakley had not told Beatriz he was leaving, had not paid her, had not bothered to get in touch with the Neatherleys, and had emptied the safe, then surely a reasonable conclusion was that he'd left suddenly. So how likely was it to be that it was merely coincidence . . .? 'Have you searched the car?'

'No. We'd no real idea what to look for and thought it best to leave it to you lot.'

It was a four-door model and he opened each door in turn. In the glove locker there were the papers required by law to be carried, a map of the island, and a garage tab which gave the date of the last service; on the floor in front, mostly on the driver's side, were several stone chips and a sprinkling of dust; on the rear seat was an English newspaper.

He returned to his own car and brought from this the torch he always carried. He switched it on and checked the surfaces previously not readily visible and on the underneath of the steering-wheel he saw a stain, three to four centimetres long, which had the look of glossy varnish. 'There could be dried blood on the wheel,' he said, as he moved back and straightened up. If Oakley had stabbed Roig, it was very possible he had got blood on his hands; driving the car had transferred the blood to the steering-wheel.

He went round to the back of the car and opened the boot. The small interior was empty of anything but a sack which, from the circular marks on it, had been used to protect the floor from butano bottles. He shut the lid. 'That's all I can do for the moment . . . Will you do me a favour?'

'Sure, so long as it doesn't mean I actually have to do anything.'

'Get on to Traffic and tell 'em to collect this car and check it out for traces. Warn 'em there may be bloodstains on the underside of the wheel so they'll need to fit an extension before they can drive—and remind 'em to use a cover on the driving seat.'

'Will do.'

He locked the car and handed the key back. Then he made his way caterwise through the rows of parking bays to the pay-booth. Exiting cars were having to queue to pay and he waited patiently for several minutes before there was a break which enabled him to question the cashier in the booth. 'Would you have been on duty here on Tuesday, just before midday?'

'That's right.' A transistor was switched on and the pop music suddenly increased in volume; he switched off the set.

'What are the chances you can remember the man who was driving this car?' Alvarez passed across the parking ticket from the Seat.

A car drew up and the man took a ticket, inserted it in the machine in front of him, asked for sixty-five pesetas, and was given a hundred-peseta coin. After handing the driver the change, he looked briefly at the ticket Alvarez had given him. He shook his head. 'Not a hope.'

'It was an eight-year-old Seat 127.'

'Like I've just said, there's no way, not with the number of cars that come through here.'

'That's what I thought, but I had to check.'

Alvarez left the booth and crossed the road to the terminal. Inside, there was for once relative calm, but that was due to a temporary lull in flights, not because a logical system of passenger handling had been introduced.

He went to the counter at the end of the long line of check-in points which dealt with last-minute applications for tickets and the young woman, smartly dressed in Iberia costume, favoured him with a professional smile. He explained the nature of his inquiries.

'You want to know if a man, who might have called

himself Oakley, bought a late ticket for a flight out on Tuesday afternoon?'

'That's right.'

'I wasn't on duty, then, but Lucía was and she's probably in the staff room right now. I'll see if I can get hold of her.' She spoke over the internal telephone, then said to him: 'She's coming down right away.'

Right away turned out to be the best part of ten minutes. Lucía was small, pert, and she had a pair of dark brown eyes that would keep most men guessing but hoping. 'I've brought the papers for Tuesday.' She opened the folder she had been carrying. 'What was the name again?'

'It could be Oakley, but is more likely to be something else. If I remember correctly, there's nothing to stop a man giving a false name when he buys a ticket?'

'Nothing.'

'And there's no check against his passport when he hands in his luggage?'

'Only when there's a blitz on against people selling the return halves of tickets they don't intend to use themselves. But that doesn't happen very often.'

'It must be years since the last one,' said the woman behind the counter.

'And when he passes through immigration, they don't compare the name on his ticket with that on his passport?'

'Can you imagine them bothering?'

He smiled. 'So if you'd look to see if there was an Oakley? If there wasn't, I'll describe the man as best I can and maybe you'll remember him.'

'I suppose that's just possible,' she said doubtfully. 'As a matter of fact, not many people bought late tickets on Tuesday.' She opened the folder and began to run her forefinger down a printed form on which several entries had been made in ink. Almost immediately, she came to a stop. 'G. Oakley. A first-class single to Heathrow.'

'He did book in his own name!' Alvarez's voice expressed

his surprise. A man fleeing the island and wanting to cover his tracks could be expected to book a ticket under a false name. Unless that was to accord him a degree of cool logic which would not be his after committing murder . . . 'Is there any chance you can remember him sufficiently well to describe him?'

She thought back for a moment, shook her head. 'Not really. I said earlier it could be a .case of maybe, but he's just a blank, even though he was first-class.'

'Then he didn't say or do anything out of the ordinary?'

'Can't have done, can he? Not like some. We get cursed for everything that goes wrong.'

'You can say that again,' commented the woman behind the counter. 'One time I was even sworn at because Manchester was shut off by fog and the plane was diverted to Birmingham. I felt like asking the old bitch if she reckoned I had a direct line to heaven.'

Alvarez thanked them and left; as he walked away, each was boastfully detailing the rudest passenger she had had to deal with.

Salas said, over the phone: 'Have you asked London to find Oakley?'

'No, señor.'

'Why the devil not?'

'I've not had confirmation yet from the forensic lab that that is blood on the steering-wheel. What's more, I haven't spoken to Señor Braddon . . .'

'How can he be of the slightest significance?'

'Apparently Roig's secretary says he and Roig had a heated row not long before the murder . . .'

'You may accept that I am aware of the facts in the case. I will rephrase the question in a simpler form. Have you evidence to suggest that Braddon knows Oakley?'

'No, I haven't.'

'Do you favour the theory that Oakley's sudden, unexpected disappearance from the island has nothing to do with the murder?'

'I'm sure it has everything to do with it.'

'Then would you agree that the pattern of Oakley's departure is that of a man panicking and desperately trying to escape before the police catch up with him?'

'Yes. Except . . .'

'Except what?'

'Why did he book in his own name?'

'Have you not just agreed he was in a state of panic?'

'But wouldn't someone in that degree of panic almost certainly draw attention to himself in one way or another? Yet the woman who sold him the ticket can't begin to remember him.'

'It hasn't occurred to you that probably her mind was filled with boyfriends and not the work she was paid to be doing?'

'Even so, a man who's really in a panic . . .'

'You know what you're trying to do, don't you?' shouted Salas.

'What, señor?'

'Complicate; complicate everything to the point where a straight line runs over itself.'

'It's just that I'd feel happier if I checked these other points and had a clearer picture of what happened.'

'Clearer picture? Show you the *Mona Lisa* and you'd see *Guernica* . . . Get on to London immediately and ask them to find Oakley. Is that clear enough to prevent you telexing New York for information on Fray Junípero Serra?'

CHAPTER 8

Lying in bed on Sunday morning, staring up at the ceiling, Alvarez tried to understand why it was that sometimes he was such a fool? Salas was satisfied the case was open and shut, so why couldn't he accept that? Yet here he was, on a day of rest, trying to decide whether or not to motor over to Magalluf to talk to the Braddons. What if there had been a row between them and Roig? It sounded as if Roig had been a man with whom it had been difficult not to have a row. And Braddon had never been seen within the vicinity of Casa Gran, nor was there any evidence to suggest he'd fled the island in panicky haste . . .

It was his peasant background which was responsible for his refusal to think sensibly, he decided. A peasant, a plodder, so often did not have the wit even to understand the uselessness of his work. When it was time to sow, but the land was too sodden, he waited with bovine patience for it to dry out; his crop grew and then the hail flattened it, the mould withered it, the mole crickets ate it, but he still tended what was left, even though it was now obvious even to him that he could never hope to gain an honest return for his work . . . And in the fullness of time, he harvested a tithe of a crop and stupidly rejoiced that he had harvested anything . . .

Arnold Braddon had opened a grocery shop in Amhurst, Hampshire, in 1897, the year of the Diamond Jubilee. He called it Braddon & Son, which was his only deliberate act of deception in an honest life—at that time he had been unmarried and he was a man of strict morals.

Later he did marry and his wife bore him the son, Joseph; but the birth was a difficult one and in consequence of the complications she was unable to have any more children. Arnold Braddon, respected if not really liked by all who knew him, died suddenly at the age of sixty-one.

From his father, Joseph Braddon inherited an overwhelming respect for honesty and a short temper, from his mother a stubbornness that at times became almost blind unreason. That the shop not only managed to survive the advent of supermarkets, but did so profitably, was due in part to his honesty—no customer was ever cheated, even indirectly, of a single penny—but far more to his stubbornness. Between them, he and his father had traded for many years and so he was not going to change anything, however many experts proved that there was no longer any room for the traditionally run grocer. For a time it had, in fact, seemed the experts were right and his customers, faced with prices higher than elsewhere, would dwindle in number until he was forced to close, but still he refused to sack most of the staff and instal self-service. Then, just in time, there was a reaction from the packaged take-it-or-leave-it of the supermarkets and people returned to favouring a shop, even if it was more expensive, where an assistant welcomed them by name, complimented them on their choices of cheese, offered them one of ten different teas, and suggested they try a newly arrived delicacy. He was, of course, fortunate that Amhurst lay in a prosperous part of the country.

His wife, Letitia, had had no children (not for want of trying; in the early days of their marriage, her enthusiasm had surprised and often embarrassed him) and so there had been no son to pass the business on to. On his retirement, he had had to sell. And the price he had been offered—for the site, not the business, much to his sorrow—had been far greater than he'd expected. By his standards, he was wealthy. He'd looked forward to a quiet, respectable retirement . . .

This was when Letitia had dropped her bombshell. Being so honest, if ever asked he would have admitted that he'd never really understood her—which was, perhaps, why they'd been happy together. Among other things, he'd always assumed that like him her roots were too firmly entrenched locally ever to be moved. But suddenly, without a single hint previously given, she'd told him she no longer wanted to live in their small, rather gloomy Edwardian house with a garden darkened by laurel bushes, but wanted to move to a large, modern, and wholly cheerful home in the

sun with a garden filled with cannas, hibiscus, oleander . . .
Live abroad? Where nobody washed, women didn't shave
under their armpits, and everyone ate garlic . . .

They'd hired a car and toured Mallorca and looked at
property for sale. The fourth house they saw had three
bedrooms, three bathrooms, central heating, an integral
garage, a swimming pool, and a garden filled with extravagant colour. 'That's for us,' she'd said. He had tried to make
her change her mind and when she'd demanded to know
what was wrong with so beautiful a place, he had stum-
blingly admitted that it was just too luxurious for an
ex-grocer . . . 'There aren't any sumptuary laws these days,'
she'd said, making it very clear that they were going to buy
the place.

He'd been so right, though for the wrong reason. The first
cracks had appeared the year after they'd moved in. He'd
complained to the builder, who hadn't been able to understand the problem; all houses cracked. Since he, along with
most other builders on the island, was an off-duty waiter, his
puzzlement was easily understood. The cracks had increased
and worsened and it became clear that the house was
suffering the effects of subsidence.

He'd consulted Roig to see if he could claim compensation
from anyone. Roig had greeted him with smiling friendliness, listened to his tale of woe, and assured him that every
house was insured for ten years from completion through
the insurances compulsorily held by architect, aparejador,
and builder.

'Do not distress yourself for one second, Señor Braddon.
We write letters to the architect, the aparejador, and the
builder, they show these to their insurance companies, and
the companies agree to the work being done.'

As they'd left the building, Letitia had said: 'There you
are, Joe. I told you there was no need to get in such a state.'

Such had been the force of Roig's assurances that for a
time Braddon had believed she was right.

The cracks opened up and spread in the summer when the earth dried out, closed in the winter once the rains had come. Repeatedly, he'd returned to Roig's office, demanding to know when something would be started.

'Señor Braddon, calm yourself. I give you my full assurance, everything is well. I have spoken to the architect and all he now needs is a more detailed letter of complaint. This he will show to his insurers and they will authorize the work.' 'Yes, you are quite right, Señor Braddon, the insurance does run for only ten years from completion, but as you have started proceedings, that time has been stopped.' 'Yes, Señor Braddon, I am doing everything that can possibly be done.'

There had been the preliminary hearing, designed to discover whether the parties could come together and reach an agreement. The lawyers for the other side had denied everything and the only consequence of the action that Braddon had ever been able to discover was that he was presented with a bill for the court fees.

There'd been the need to photograph the cracks for the court records. After they were taken, a notario had had to certify the photographs were a true likeness of the cracks; another eighty-odd thousand pesetas . . .

'I know he was only in your house for fifteen minutes, Señor Braddon, but notarios are always expensive. We have a saying, "If you wish to dine off silver plates, become a politician; if off gold ones, a notario."'

And then, one morning in March, Braddon had gone to Roig's office for the umpteenth time to try to get someone to do something, and the secretary had said—in her fractured, hesitant English—that she was sorry, but Señor Roig was out; however, it was fortunate that the señor had called as there was a letter for him. It proved to be brief and to the point. Roig was very sorry, but he could no longer act for Señor Braddon since his wife was cousin to the aparejador's wife and it was not right to go to law against one's own family.

When, almost incoherent with rage, he'd shown the letter to a friend, he'd learned just how devious Roig had been. In order to make a valid claim against the architect, the aparejador, and the builder, it was necessary within the ten years to bring an action in the courts. Yet despite all Roig's encouraging reports, no step had been taken which, in this context, started the action; that could only happen when certain papers were signed and deposited.

'Then what happens about the time-limit?'

'Since the case hasn't started, you've got to get those papers deposited as soon as possible and before the ten years are up.'

'But they are almost up.'

'Are you quite certain you didn't sign anything asking for the case to be brought?'

'Roig never told me I had to; he kept saying that everything which had to be done, had been.'

'He obviously meant you.'

Braddon had not found that amusing.

Nor had he been amused when he discovered that he could not call in another solicitor until he had paid the bill of Roig; in other words, pay him for all the work he had not done. He finally understood why the island's lawyers were called the Mafia by the general public.

CHAPTER 9

Alvarez felt sorry for Braddon and wondered why he'd ever been so ill-advised as to come and live on the island? It was so obvious that he was far too unworldly ever to be able to meet a cunning peasant on equal terms.

'He swindled me,' said Braddon furiously.

'Yes, dear,' said Letitia, 'but nothing you can say or do now will alter what's happened so there's not really much point in going on and on about it, is there?'

'If this were England, I could drag him through the courts and see him struck off the Rolls.'

'But we aren't in England.'

'And whose bloody fault is that?'

'Señor,' said Alvarez, hoping to outflank a domestic row, 'after receiving that letter, did you return to Señor Roig's office?'

'I did. And I told him just what I goddamn well thought of him . . .'

'Joe,' said Letitia, 'do try and calm down; it's not good for you to get so excited.'

'How did he react to what you said?' asked Alvarez.

'Didn't like it when I told him he was nothing but a lousy crook.'

'Joe sometimes becomes excited,' she said, obviously far more aware of the potentially dangerous significance of what he was saying than he, 'but it never lasts . . . Joe, wouldn't it be an idea to have some drinks?'

For a moment it looked as if Braddon would ignore the suggestion, but then he stood. He asked what they'd like to drink, left, crossing the patio into the house.

Even if they did have problems with the foundations of the house, thought Alvarez, they'd a very desirable property. Their own land all round them and the next house a couple of hundred metres away, views of both the mountains and the sea . . .

'The trouble with Joe is that he's so completely straight-forward.'

Alvarez looked at her as she sat in the shade of a sun umbrella. At first, he'd been inclined to regard her as meek and colourless; now, he appreciated that behind the quiet appearance and manner there was considerable determination.

'And because he's like that, he's never ready for anyone who's devious. And if that person takes advantage of him, he feels betrayed. Can you understand what I'm trying to say?'

'Indeed, señora.'

'I had a feeling about Roig from the beginning. Maybe it was because he always smiled with his mouth, but never with his eyes. Joe could never see that. If he takes to a person, he won't hear anything against him; and he thinks people he likes are every bit as honest as himself. Every time there was another delay, I suggested we ought to speak to someone else to make certain that Roig really was doing everything he should. Joe said that that would be disloyal to him.

'Then, when Roig as good as admitted he'd been stringing us along to protect his relations, Joe was not only shocked and hurt, but also very worried because if the repairs cost four million, which is what a builder suggested, we're going to have to dig into capital and he's a horror of doing that although we'd still be well off and we've no one to leave our money to. So it was worry as much as anything which made him talk like he did. But his anger never lasts. And the way he's talking now is because of worry and not . . . I mean, you can't believe . . .'

'What can't I believe, señora?'

She shook her head, afraid to put into words a possibility which—as unlikely as this might be—he had perhaps not yet determined for himself.

Braddon, carrying a tray, returned to the patio. He passed the glasses, then sat. His chair was in the full sun and after a few seconds he pulled a handkerchief from his pocket and mopped his brow.

'Why don't you move into the shade?' she suggested.

'I'm all right.'

'But you'll roast if you stay there and you know how easily you burn.'

'Stop fussing.'

So stubborn, thought Alvarez, that he'd rather suffer

unnecessary discomfort than be seen to change his mind. Would he stubbornly go on hating? . . . 'Señor, as I said at the beginning, I would be grateful if you would answer some questions.'

'I know nothing about the murder; nothing at all. But I'll tell you one thing: I'm not shedding any tears over it.'

'Don't talk like that,' she said, her voice high.

'Why not?'

'Because it's stupid.'

'It's stupid to think a man changes his character just because he dies.'

Alvarez asked: 'When was the last time you saw him?'

'When I told him in his office precisely what I thought of him.'

'Have you ever been to his country home, Casa Gran?'

'Never been on visiting terms, not even before I realized what kind of a man he was. I didn't even know he'd got that place until I read it's where he was killed. I suppose he bought it out of what he'd made from mugs like us.'

'I imagine you own a car—what make is it?'

'A Renault eleven.'

'And does the señora also have one?'

'I've an old Panda to do the shopping in,' she answered. 'Why do you want to know?'

'A car was seen driving up to Casa Gran on the afternoon of the murder and I have to try and identify whose it was.'

'If we didn't know he owned the place, it couldn't very well be either of our cars, could it?' said Braddon belligerently.

'Joe, the Inspector has to ask questions,' she said, trying to awaken her husband to the fact that it obviously wasn't in his interests to antagonize a policeman.

Braddon finished his drink, put the glass down on the cane table with unnecessary force. 'Do you think I murdered him?'

She gasped at this fresh stupidity.

Alvarez said evenly: 'Did you, señor?'

'No. But like I said, whoever did has my vote. He was nothing but a swindler.'

'And you believe that that warrants his being murdered?'

She spoke hurriedly. 'Joe often says things he doesn't mean.'

'I mean exactly . . .' began Braddon.

She suddenly pointed up into the sky. 'There's an Eleonora's falcon.' They watched the bird as it gracefully curved in flight. 'I saw an osprey three days ago and it had a fish in its talons. There's a wonderful range of raptors out here.'

It had been a brave attempt to turn the conversation away from dangerous subjects and Alvarez was sorry to have to cut it short. 'Señor, will you tell me where you were last Monday night?'

'I said, I didn't kill him.'

'I still need to know where you were.'

'Here.'

'Is there someone who can confirm that?'

'I can,' she said loudly.

'And perhaps there is also someone else? Do you have a maid who lives in?'

'We have a daily woman, that's all.'

'Did any friends call?'

They looked at each other; she answered. 'There's no one came to see us Monday night.'

CHAPTER 10

Palma was a city which was often denigrated, usually by people who had never visited the island on the grounds that their hairdressers went there every year. But for those who did not have to be seen by their friends to holiday in Pago Pago, it had much to offer and in parts was charmingly attractive.

Alvarez parked in a newly vacated space, climbed out of
the car and stood on the pavement, admiring the setting.
Behind him was a small green, ringed with palm trees, off
which there led a broad road which provided a brief view
of the boat-filled marina; ahead of him was a church, in
parts nearly five hundred years old, which was simple yet
graceful in style, but had sombre associations with the
Inquisition; and to his right was Bistro Deux, a French
restaurant whose reputation was excellent.

He crossed, walked past the church and down a side road
that curved around rising land. He stopped at a block of
flats, checked the names by the entryphone, pressed the
third button down. A woman, her voice made tinny by the
loudspeaker, answered. He identified himself. There was a
sharp buzz and the door sprang open. He went in and
crossed to the lift.

When Raquel Oliver opened the door, he was immediately reminded of Jaume's contemptuous certainty that
Roig's women were far from innocent; undoubtedly, she
was. Strikingly attractive, she made the mistake of being
too obvious; hair very blonde, make-up very heavy, shirt
and jeans very tight, and air of hard calculation unmistakable.

'Well,' she said, 'd'you reckon you'll know me the next
time?'

'I am sorry, señorita, I was just . . .' He became silent,
deeming it imprudent to explain that he had just unflatter-
ingly summed up her character.

She accepted that his regard had been wholly lecherous.
'I suppose you'd better come in.'

It was a small flat, built for a single person or a newly-wed
couple. She had furnished it with a striking and artistic
recourse to colours, many of which when apart might have
been thought to clash, but when placed together astonish-
ingly didn't.

'D'you want a drink?'

'If I might have a coñac, with just ice?'

He watched her go over to a small sideboard. An islander, probably from the western end to judge by the accent with which she spoke Mallorquin. Had she been born forty years before, her life would have been a very different one. Forced to work in the fields from an early age, by now her looks would have disappeared; married to a man who probably offered her little or no overt affection; facing a future, as hard as the past, in which pleasure was a privilege restricted to the wealthy . . . Who but the severest of moralists could regret the change for her?

'I'll tell you one thing, you're no chatterbox!'

'I was thinking about the past, señorita.'

'That's a complete waste of time.' She handed him a glass, went over to the second easy chair whose cover was a shocking pink, and sat. 'I suppose you're here because of Pablo?'

'I believe you visited him quite often at his house, Casa Gran?'

'And if I did?'

'Then you can tell me about him.'

'What about him?'

'To begin with, what was he like?'

'Like any other middle-aged man who imagines he's Don Juan,' she said, making it clear that she was not going to apologize to anyone, least of all to a middle-aged inspector, for the kind of life she led. She'd met Roig at an exhibition to which she'd gone because she knew the artist. She'd recognized his type on sight and so wasn't in the least surprised when he'd made a point of talking to her. And she'd been sardonically amused to note how he'd preened himself, believing that his sophisticated air, hundred thousand peseta suit, and hand-made shoes, would bowl her over. Naturally, she'd played hard to get. She'd made him spend and spend on her and for a long time had offered absolutely nothing in return . . . She could not quite hide

the fact that his mature charm had held an attraction for
her.

'Were you distressed to learn of his death?'

'Of course. No more dinners at the Casino.'

He ignored the comment. 'How did you learn of his
death?'

'I read about it in the paper. Bit of a surprise, really. To
think that suddenly he'd . . .' Just for a moment, her air of
hard sophistication was dropped.

'You'd no idea what had happened until then?'

'How could I have?' Her concern was sharp. 'Here, you're
not thinking I had anything to do with that?'

'I'm here to find out.'

'Then you find out bloody quickly. If you think I could
ever have stuck a knife into him, you're crazy . . . I mean,
why the hell should I kill him?'

'You might have had a very bitter argument.'

'D'you think I murder people I argue with? . . . In any
case, when we went to his place, it wasn't to argue.'

'Or you might have learned he'd found another
friend?'

'He wasn't looking at anyone else while I was around,
that was for sure.'

'When did you last see him?'

She thought back. 'On the Friday.'

'Have you any idea who might have killed him?'

'No.' She drained her glass, stood. 'D'you want another?'

He handed her his glass. 'He never spoke about being
threatened?'

'That's not the sort of talk he was interested in,' she said,
as she walked over to the sideboard.

'It's strange what does get said in pillow talk.'

'Not when I'm sharing the pillow.'

'I suppose you've met the maid at Casa Gran?'

'Couldn't very well miss that one.' She walked back,
handed him a glass, returned to her chair. 'Every time I

looked like getting too close so she might actually come into physical contact, she crossed herself.'

'Did she ever talk to you about Roig?'

'She didn't talk to me about anyone or anything unless she absolutely had to.'

'So I don't suppose you'd know who he—how shall I put it?—entertained before?'

'That's right, I wouldn't.'

'Can you remember where you were on Monday evening, say between ten and midnight?'

She answered immediately. 'Here, watching a film on telly.'

'On your own.'

'On my own, so you can cool your imagination.'

'I have to ask the question, to learn if there is someone who will corroborate that you were here.'

'Well, there isn't, so you'll just have to . . . Hang on. A friend did phone me during the film and as it was boring, we had a bit of a chat.'

'Would you give me his or her name?'

'Hers.'

He wrote down the name, telephone number, and address. He finished his drink, thanked her for her help, said goodbye, and left.

There was a pay-telephone in Bistro Deux and after giving his order—which called for a great deal of thought because the menu was full and promising and he did not want to regret his choice later—he telephoned the woman whose name he'd been given. She confirmed the telephone conversation and was able to place the time at around eleven.

Back in his seat, he poured himself out a glass of wine, sprinkled olive oil and salt on a slice of bread, and ate and drank as he thought. Two things were clear: assuming the friend was not an accomplice, Raquel had a reasonably good alibi; and when Julia had railed against Roig for destroying innocence, she had not had Raquel in mind.

*

Roig's town house in Palma had been built a couple of centuries before for an ancient, and near noble, Madrileño family who, in much state, had visited the island for holidays. The rooms, all large and with lofty ceilings, were built around an inner courtyard; with the heavy, studded outside doors shut, this courtyard had, before it had been paved to provide parking space, offered a touch of the countryside in the middle of the town.

Despite the heat, Elena Roig was dressed in full mourning, as had been customary until recently. She accepted Alvarez's condolences and his apologies for worrying her at such a time and then cleared away any hurdle of embarrassment by saying: 'I knew my husband owned this house in the country and that he entertained women there. But I don't think he ever realized that I knew.' She briefly touched a large mole on her right cheek. Age had softened her ugliness, and for that she was grateful, but it could not hide it; and for her, that unsightly mole had always epitomized her unfortunate appearance.

'Did you by any chance meet any of these women, señora?'

'Certainly not.'

'So you obviously cannot give me any of their names?'

'I cannot.'

'Did you often meet his friends?'

'If now you are referring to his male friends, only when he hoped they'd be able to persuade me.'

'In what way?'

'When I was very much younger, I inherited considerable land and some property. Part of that I immediately put in his hands as a sign of trust—one can be very naïve when one is young—the rest I retained in my own name. The land especially has appreciated greatly in value and he was forever trying to make me agree to let him have some or all of it to sell. His friends, who were always in the business of developing, were introduced to me in order to lend weight to his pleas. My response was always the same and it always angered him.' She spoke with such detachment that he might have been no more than the most casual of acquaintances. 'The trouble was that he could never understand why I should turn down the chance of such enormous profits. But if I have enough money to live on, why should I allow even more land to be destroyed merely in order to become unnecessarily richer?'

'I would that more people had thought like you over the past years, señora.' As he finished speaking, she turned and looked directly at him and in the subdued light—the house still retained the original small windows—her large brown eyes were lustrous and he was suddenly struck by how beautiful they were and how at variance with the rest of her face.

'You're about the same age as me. Then you can also remember the island before the foreigners came. Everything was so beautiful then,' she said sadly.

Indeed, the island had been very beautiful. But the people had known poverty and he could remember his mother crying because she could not give him a decent meal.

'What are you thinking?'

He told her.

'That's true. Must it always, then, be either beauty with want or ugly prosperity?'

It was a question he had often asked himself and to which he had never found an answer.

'Pablo could never think like that.' Her tone had scarcely changed, but now there was no mistaking her contempt. 'For him, beauty was success and money. And young women.' She touched the mole.

'Señora, have you ever met an Englishman called Gerald Oakley?'

'I don't think so.'

'I'm reasonably certain he visited Casa Gran on Monday.'

'It's possible. On Sunday, Pablo once more tried to per-

suade me to let him have some of the land; he was even
more insistent than usual. Perhaps the Englishman was
interested in the development of it.'

'But he didn't actually mention Oakley's name?'

'No, he did not.'

'Has he sold all the land you gave him?'

'A long time ago. And for very much less than it would
be worth now, as I frequently pointed out, much to his
annoyance.'

'Was he ever concerned in the actual developments?'

'I can't say. He never discussed money or business with
me, unless he wanted something; and even then, like any
husband, he'd speak as if I were a fool.'

Few Mallorquins, Alvarez knew, had yet come to terms
either with the proposition that a marriage was a partnership
rather than a takeover or that women could be as intelli-
gently capable of dealing with financial matters as they.

He stood, apologized once more for having troubled her,
and said goodbye. As he stepped out of the cool interior of
the house into the hot, dusty street, he thought that it was
like returning to the present.

On Monday, Alvarez drove again to Palma and parked
under the Plaza Major. From there, he walked to Roig's
office, on the first floor of a building in Rey Jaime III.

The reception area was large, close-carpeted, and hung
with several attractive coloured prints; the single desk was
kidney-shaped. Marta had been working at a large electronic
typewriter and she immediately began to moan. 'I just don't
know what to do. I mean, who's employing me? There's a
lot of work needs doing, but who's going to pay me for doing
it? And the phone's been going all the time with questions
I can't answer.'

As if on cue, the telephone rang. She told the caller that
just for the moment she couldn't say definitely what was
happening, but that the delay wouldn't affect the case; she

promised to get in touch the moment something certain was known.

She replaced the receiver. 'I've tried asking the señora, but I don't think she can be bothered. Between you and me, she and the señor didn't get on very well together.'

'I gather he was fond of the ladies?'

'All I know is, he'd wandering hands.'

'D'you remember the Braddons?'

'Not likely to forget 'em.'

'Why not?'

'If you'd been here the last time, you wouldn't ask.'

He did not immediately pursue what she'd said. 'Were they frequent callers?'

'Never stopped.'

'They were trying to make Señor Roig expedite their action over the house they bought, weren't they?'

'That's right.'

'D'you have any idea why he didn't press their claim harder?'

'Because he was stringing 'em along until it was all but too late for them to sue.'

'You knew he was doing that?'

'I'm not stupid.'

'Then why didn't you warn them?'

'I was working for him, not them; besides, they're foreigners.'

'Going back to their last visit here, what happened?'

'There was a row like no other I've heard in this office; leastwise, the English señor was shouting his head off.'

'What was it all about?'

'It must have been to do with the letter I'd typed out a couple of days before, saying the señor wouldn't be able to act for them any longer.'

'Could you understand what Señor Braddon was saying?'

'Not really. He was shouting too fast and a lot of the words I didn't know.'

'So you wouldn't be able to say if he'd made any threats?'

'It sounded as if it was nothing but threats.'

'But you can't be certain?'

'No,' she said reluctantly.

'I've been chatting to various people and it seems Señor Roig was interested in property as well as doing his job here. D'you know for sure if that's correct?'

'It's dead right.'

'Presumably, it was only in a small way?'

'Would you call La Portaña small?'

He whistled. 'I certainly would not. How deep was he in that?'

'I can't say. I mean, I never had anything really to do with that kind of work. But sometimes there'd be a telephone call and I'd hear . . .' She stopped. 'Well, I'd hear something before I could put the receiver down after switching the call through.'

'Yes, of course.' Alvarez sounded as if he accepted that anything she'd overheard had been done so inadvertently. 'So you heard La Portaña mentioned—can you remember what was said?'

'Only roughly, because they were talking in English and although I'm all right when people speak slowly and don't get too complicated, I can get lost—like I was with Señor Braddon that time . . . The person on the other end of the line was saying something about the banks becoming worried over the money they'd lent on La Portaña and he couldn't understand.'

'Couldn't understand what?'

'I don't really know. He began to speak really quickly. But it was something to do with where money had got to. And then Señor Roig said he'd have to get a folder and that meant his coming through here.'

Alvarez pictured her hurriedly replacing the receiver before she was caught eavesdropping. 'Do you know who the caller was?'

'He didn't give me his name; just said he wanted to speak to Señor Roig.'

'And when he was put through, he didn't identify himself?'

'Yes, he did, but I don't remember what he said; it wasn't a name I'd heard before.'

'Think back hard.'

After a moment, she shook her head. 'It's no good. I mean, foreigners have such difficult names...' She stopped.

'Yes?'

'Isn't that odd? It's funny how one's mind works.'

'You have remembered?'

'Not exactly, but it was something like...' It took her three attempts to say, 'Gerry.'

CHAPTER 11

The telephone rang and Alvarez lifted the receiver.

'Forensic here, Inspector. Thought you'd like a preliminary report on the autopsy. The deceased was killed by a stab wound delivered by knife—not that there was ever any doubt on that score. Although we can never be certain, death was probably virtually instantaneous.

'The knife used is shorter than the depth of the wound which suggests the upward blow was delivered with considerable force, compressing the wall of the body just below the ribs. In addition to this, the very ragged nature and width of the wound suggest that the knife was withdrawn, probably only partially, and then thrust home again at least once. In our opinion, this rules out any defence that death was not intended.

'One more thing. I've had a word with the lab boys and they've asked me to pass on to you the fact that it's confirmed that the only prints on the knife are those of the daily woman.'

'Was the murderer wearing gloves, then?'

'I gather, not necessarily. The knife has a thin handle, considering the length of the blade, and so the murderer's fingers may well have wrapped right round it and the tips rested on the flesh of the hand.'

'Anything to make things more difficult.'

'That's right,' agreed the assistant unsympathetically.

Alvarez stopped the car by a large hoarding on which blue letters against a bright red background declared that La Portaña was the finest urbanización on the island, and stepped out on to the road. The land, which had been well wooded, sloped gently upwards from the sea in a wedge shape; it was roughly fifty hectares in all. Beyond, on either side, although this was screened by the shape of the land and narrow belts of trees, was heavily developed and so it was obvious that this land had been owned by someone who had held on to it long after the start of the building boom; equally obviously, he or she had finally decided it was impossible any longer to forgo the immense profit to be had by selling it.

As was required by law—although often carefully forgotten—roads had been built, electric cables run to junction boxes, water pipes laid, and street lights installed, before any building had been started. Now, several houses and two blocks of flats were under construction; the houses were obviously going to be large and the blocks of flats no more than four storeys high and—most unusually—of an attractive design with flowing curves. In the centre of the urbanización was a public garden and this was ringed with mature palm trees, transplanted from near Valencia; there were also grass, green from generous watering, and flowerbeds bright with colour.

Alvarez returned to the car and drove down to the wooden

building which was being used as the sales office, close to the main entrance of the urbanización. He went inside. A narrow room ran the length of the building and in this were two desks, a counter on which were set out sales brochures and reprints of an article which had appeared in an international glossy magazine, and a frame on an easel on which was a large-scale plan of the development.

A young man who had been seated at the desk nearer to the counter finally came to his feet. He had a spiky hairstyle and a very prominent Adam's apple and his pink shirt did not rest comfortably with his puce slacks. He eyed Alvarez with supercilious disdain, correctly judging it unlikely a sale was in the offing.

'Cuerpo general de policia.'

The young man's expression became watchful, though perhaps even more supercilious.

'I'd like a word with whoever's in charge.'

Vich's office lay behind the general room and was half the size of that. He was a small, slightly built man, with an outgoing manner. He shook hands, then moved a chair away from the wall to the front of the desk. 'So how can I help you?' he asked as he sat behind the desk.

'I need to know who owns the urbanización?'

'It's a company—Andreu y Soler.'

'Was Pablo Roig connected with it?'

Vich was surprised. 'How d'you know that?'

'Shouldn't I, then?'

'Well, I'll put it like this—it's not a secret, but his name doesn't appear in the general literature . . . It was one hell of a shock to hear he'd been murdered. That's why you're here now?'

Alvarez nodded.

'Then you reckon there may be some connection between the murder and this company?'

'There's the possibility. What I want to try and find out is if there's a probability.'

Vich shook his head. 'I don't see how there can be.'

'Let's start by you giving me a broad picture of the set-up here.'

Vich spoke briskly, suggesting a well-informed, decisive man. Andreu y Soler had been formed specifically to buy the land and develop the urbanización of La Portaña. Roig had been the company's legal adviser and it was he who had managed to obtain planning permission even though the land had originally been classified green belt. In addition, all the original working capital had come through his hands, although there was no suggestion that he had personally provided it.

'I gather that recently finance has become a problem?'

Vich's expression changed. 'What makes you say that?'

Alvarez smiled briefly. 'We all have our secrets. Yours is how planning permission was given, mine is the source of my information.'

Vich picked up a pencil and fiddled with it. 'Suppose I tell you that any report about a financial problem is an exaggeration?'

'Then I'll know that the company is in deep trouble.'

'No, not deep . . . Look, I suppose everything I tell you is confidential?'

'Of course.'

'Well, there are problems. Once we obtained planning permission we needed extra capital and went to the banks for it—that, in fact, was the intention from the beginning. All the sums had been done, but almost inevitably costs have risen above the estimates—for one thing, the latest wage rise was twice what we'd projected. Oil sheiks have become very thin on the ground and that leaves a big hole in the number of people willing to pay ten thousand pesetas a square metre.'

'Is that what the land costs?' asked Alvarez in astonishment.

'That's right.'

'I wonder you've sold any at all . . . So what's been happening about this?'

'There's been a search for fresh capital.'

'By whom?'

'The holding company, I guess.'

'What holding company?'

'Ashley Developments. It's registered in the Cayman Islands. Obviously, the original capital came through them. They set up Andreu y Soler here with the Spanish directors holding only the minimum number of shares required by Spanish company law.'

'It sounds as if there'll be one hell of a job unravelling the knots if the urbanización goes bust.'

'There's no call to talk about going bust, Inspector,' said Vich hastily. 'All that we have is a temporary cashflow problem. When that's solved the banks will be happy and the development will go right ahead as planned and will be highly profitable. I know I said a bit earlier on that the plots haven't been selling all that quickly, but that doesn't mean the outlook's gloomy. We're in a very strong position, really, because we're offering something which is becoming rarer and rarer: exclusiveness.'

'You're beginning to sound like a salesman!'

Vich laughed. 'Nonsense—I'm telling you the truth . . . It's like this. When the rich buy a home, whether it's to live in or just for holidays, they demand two things: that the property tells everyone else they're rich and that they're well protected from the non-rich. Here, we can offer them both. Anyone who buys a plot of land of a minimum size of four thousand square metres at ten thousand a metre, on which the house that is built must cost at least forty million, has to be rich; and in the near future, the whole urbanización will be surrounded by a security fence in which there'll be only two gates, each of which will be manned twenty-four hours a day. The rich may not find it easy to get through the eye of a needle, but the poor will sure as hell find it impossible to enter here.'

'Sounds more like a prison.'

'Aren't we all, in fact, in some sort of prison?'

'If I listen to you much longer, suicide will come as a relief.'

Vich smiled.

'Let's leave the rich to enjoy their exclusive riches. What can you tell me about the company in the Cayman Islands?'

'Nothing.'

'Come off it.'

'That's the plain truth. The only contact I've ever had with them is through cheques; and the signature on those has always been an illegible scrawl.'

'How much d'you reckon they've invested?'

Vich leaned back in his chair and joined the tips of the fingers of his two hands together. 'That's a very sensitive figure.'

'So's my continuing goodwill. I told you, the conversation is confidential.'

Vich picked up the pencil and wrote down a series of figures, did a few quick calculations, then said: 'Call it five billion pesetas and you won't be far out.'

'That's excluding borrowings from the banks?'

'That's right. Makes the mind boggle, doesn't it? Teaches you how the other half of the world lives.'

'Not a very edifying lesson. Does the name of Gerald or Gerry Oakley say anything to you?'

'No.'

'Then that's that.' Alvarez stood.

Vich looked up. 'I've given you a fair bit of information, but not received any at all in return. Who is Oakley and how could he be connected with here? How could Andreu y Soler have anything to do with the murder of Roig?'

'At the moment, I've not the slightest idea.'

Vich's expression called him a liar.

*

London telephoned at five twenty-five that afternoon. Reference the request for information concerning an Englishman, Gerald Oakley, who had travelled first class from Palma to London on flight IB 628 on the ninth of the month. Regretfully, on the scant information provided, it had proved impossible to trace him.

'It would,' said the inspector, who spoke very passable Spanish, 'help considerably if you could furnish us with something more definite—say, the number of his passport.'

'At the moment,' replied Alvarez, 'we don't have any details. He's a casual visitor, never staying for very long, and so he's not had to apply for a permanencia or residencia; he's a sub-tenant and neither he nor the man who owns the lease has ever bothered to have any legal agreement drawn up; he's never used any of the local banks. So we've no record of his passport number or, for that matter, of any other documents. On top of that, friends seemed to have learned very little about him.'

'Would you say he's been deliberately covering his tracks?'

'I've been thinking about that and in this connection I'm sure it's significant that in his house there isn't a single piece of paper with any personal information on it.'

'This is beginning to look interesting! When your request reached us, we naturally circulated the details through all departments and county forces in the usual way. In the past few hours, I've heard from the Fraud Squad. They've nothing definite against Oakley, but his name has surfaced in a current investigation and they wanted to question him, but discovered he'd left no trace of his present whereabouts . . . Can you give me a fuller breakdown of his possible connection with the murder case?'

Alvarez detailed what was known

'If he's in business in Mallorca, that ties up—speaking very generally—with things here. The Fraud Squad's

interested in a heavy case of insider dealing. D'you know
what I mean by that?'

'Isn't it something to do with shares?'

'It's using confidential information to buy stock that's
about to rise. On the Exchange they say it's clever buying
if you're not caught, insider dealing if you are. Anyway, the
crux of the matter is that recently a couple of clerks from
different firms were chatting and they discovered that on
several occasions there'd been heavy orders to buy shares
in a company which had soon afterwards been the subject
of a takeover bid, whereupon the shares had soared upwards.
It smelled like insider dealing, so they reported their sus-
picions to their bosses. The Department of Trade and Indus-
try were called in and after a while their investigators alerted
the Fraud Squad. A suspect was turned up who works
in one of the merchant banks concerned in the contested
takeover bids. Unfortunately, there is so far absolutely no
direct evidence of his involvement. The information can be
shown to have been available to him, if never exclusively to
him, but not that he's ever done more with the information
than he was supposed to. The share dealings were isolated,
of course, but none of them was carried out in his name or
in the name of anyone with whom he can be shown to have
the slightest connection. His financial affairs have been very
closely investigated and there's not been a penny spent or
invested which he can't legitimately account for. So to date
it's a case of probability without proof.'

'Surely the name of the buyer or buyers of the shares
helps?'

'In every case it was a company, registered in the Cayman
Islands. Under their present laws, no bank, company, or
other financial institution, can be forced to reveal any evidence to a third party except in circumstances in which
there has been an action committed which amounts to a
crime both there and in the country seeking information. In
the Cayman Islands, insider dealing is not a criminal

offence. Which is hardly surprising since they don't have a stock exchange.'

'What's the name of the company?'

There was a pause. 'I did read it, but dammit, I've forgotten.'

'Ashley Developments, by any chance?'

'I've an idea that that's precisely what it was! How have you come across it?'

'Andreu y Soler is developing an urbanización here and the original capital was provided by Ashley Developments, which set up the Spanish company. Roig, the murdered man, was legal adviser to Andreu y Soler and it was also through him that much of the money passed. Oakley had a heated row with Roig in the late afternoon of the day of the murder.'

'The Fraud Squad is going to like this!'

They spoke for a couple of minutes about other matters —in particular, the weather—and had begun to say goodbye when the inspector interrupted himself. 'I almost forgot. I don't know if it's of any direct importance to you, but one of the first-class passengers never showed on that flight.'

'Can the passenger be identified?'

'Not a hope this end. It's the usual situation. The airline had a list of passengers, but there was no check on the names of those who boarded.'

'Well, I'd say there's one thing that's certain—it wasn't Oakley who failed to turn up!'

'Not if you're right in your surmises. He'd have flown the plane himself in order to escape from the island.'

A couple of minutes later, the call was concluded. Alvarez hesitated, then phoned Salas.

'So far as we're concerned, then,' said Salas, 'there's nothing more we can do and it's up to England to find Oakley?'

'That's the way it looks, señor.'

'Then that's the way it's damned well going to stay.'

*

Palma telephoned at seven-fifteen, shortly before Alvarez had decided to finish work.

'Forensic lab here. We've examined the interior of the Seat 127, registration number PM 12050. The stains on the steering-wheel are dried blood. In addition, further stains, though very much fainter, were found on the back seat and on the rubber mat on the floor at the back—attempts had almost certainly been made to wash both seat and mat. All three stains were of group O which is, of course, the commonest.'

Alvarez fiddled with a strand of hair as he tried to picture the scene. In stabbing Roig to death, Oakley had got blood on his hands. But while it was easy to see how he then transferred this to the steering-wheel, how had there come to be blood in the back of the car? Had Oakley also got blood on his clothes and shoes and had he for some reason climbed into the back of the car? Why, when every second counted if he was to escape from the island? And why hadn't he also stained the front seat of the car? . . .

'Are you still there?'

'I'm sorry,' he said hurriedly. 'I was thinking.'

'There's one other thing. The blood of the deceased is group B.'

'But . . . but that's impossible.'

'Sorry. There's no room for any doubt.'

The full meaning of what he had just been told swept through his mind and with sinking heart he realized he was going to have to telephone Salas. He reached down to the bottom right-hand drawer of his desk and brought out the bottle of brandy and glass which he kept there for emergencies.

CHAPTER 12

Alvarez tried to speak with calm confidence. 'I think that after Oakley was murdered, his body was bundled into the back of his car and then the murderer drove off to hide it, probably in one of the remoter parts of the mountains where it is unlikely ever to be found. Inevitably, he got some blood on his hands and it was this which stained the steering-wheel. The next morning he drove the Seat to the airport and left it in the car park, went into the terminal and booked a late ticket in Oakley's name. Obviously all this was designed to make it seem that Oakley had murdered Roig and had then fled. Rightly, the real murderer reckoned that the risk of his being remembered at the airport was virtually nil.'

'What are you saying?' Salas shouted.

'Señor, I have just tried to explain . . .'

'Why should Oakley be murdered?'

'As I see it, for one of two reasons. Either because he inadvertently witnessed the murder of Roig, and so in turn had to be eliminated, or else because both he and Roig were involved in something which had to do with the development of La Portaña. I think the latter is the more probable, although I have to admit that I've no idea why their involvement should have proved so deadly.'

'I just don't believe it.'

'Señor, it is a fact that in the case there have been small, but significant, questions which haven't been answered. For instance, his position in the setting up of a development that big shows Oakley to have been an intelligent and sharp businessman. So wouldn't he have realized that to murder Roig on the same evening that he must have been overheard having a row with him was bound . . .'

'I just don't believe that in one afternoon even you can telephone me to say that Oakley is the murderer and has fled to England and then, within two hours, that Oakley isn't the murderer and hasn't fled to England, he has been murdered.'

'The thing is, when I first spoke to you I hadn't heard from Forensic regarding the blood types . . .'

'Then why the devil did you say anything until you had?'

'Señor, you insisted that I advise you immediately of every development and . . .'

'Do you begin to realize just what you've done.'

'In what particular respect, señor?'

'You're now going to have to ring the English police to say there is no need for them to search for Oakley since he is not in England and is not a murderer, he has been murdered. That will brand you a fool.'

'But if I explain . . .'

'Far worse, it brands me as a superior chief who, albeit unwillingly, commands a fool.'

'If you remember, señor, I did suggest to you that we should not contact England until we'd had confirmation from Forensic . . .'

'You said no such thing. On the contrary, I counselled caution, a counselling which you chose to ignore with inevitable results.'

The bitter injustice of this made Alvarez reach across for his glass, only to find it was empty. He looked down at the waste-paper basket, but the bottle of Soberano he'd previously emptied had not been miraculously refilled.

After a long pause, Salas continued in a voice of gloom: 'What do you intend to do after you've phoned England?'

'Continue my investigations, señor. While, as I said earlier, I lean to the motive for the two murders being connected with the development at La Portaña, I feel we cannot overlook the alternative possibility.'

'I wish that . . .' The superior chief cut short his words.

Alvarez tried not to speculate on what that wish might
have been.

When Alvarez arrived home, the family, with the exception
of Dolores who was in the kitchen, was watching television.
She appeared in the doorway. 'You're late and I've had to
do everything I can think of to try to keep the meal from
overcooking.'

'I'm sorry,' he said contritely. 'I had so much work . . .'

'And that, of course, is so much more important than
arriving back in time for the meal.'

Juan spoke petulantly. 'Mama, we're trying to listen to
the telly.'

Her voice sharpened still further. 'Which, young man,
you'll find very hard to do if I send you upstairs for being
rude.' She had been studying Alvarez and now her attitude
changed and she became concerned instead of imperiously
annoyed. 'Enrique, is something the matter?'

'No, not really. It's just that I feel worn right out.'

'Why?'

'The superior chief's been going for me. He says I've
made him look a fool.'

'God did that, not you. A drink will cheer you up and
make you forget him.'

'It certainly would, but I don't want to delay the meal
any more and ruin it.'

'Nothing will come to any harm for waiting a few moments
longer,' she replied, grandly ignoring what she had said
earlier. She turned and disappeared from sight.

Jaime stood, crossed to the large cupboard, and brought
out of it a bottle of brandy and two glasses. He spoke in a
low tone so that his voice would not carry to the kitchen. 'I
was going to have one earlier, but she told me I'd been
drinking far too much and ought to go without.' He poured
out two very generous drinks and passed one glass across.
He winked. 'Come back tired more often.'

Alvarez drove cross-country to Casa Gran; the route was slower, but it took him through countryside he loved, not least because it was so unchanged—few foreigners lived there and the destructive tide of tourism had completely passed it by. The rolling land was seldom irrigated and many of the fields grew almond trees; underneath these, flocks of sheep searched for sustenance among the sun-scorched grass and weeds. To the north were the mountains; some slopes grew pines, others were bare, and it was difficult to pick out any features to account for the difference. Above the mountains there could still occasionally be seen a black vulture, riding the sky as it searched for carrion.

He parked, crossed to the arched entrance passage and opened the door to the right. He stepped inside and called out and from a distance a woman answered. He waited patiently and eventually Julia came into the hall. When he saw her wrinkled face, leathery skin, and bowed back, he was reminded of his mother even though the two women did not look alike; a lifetime of toil on the land, stretching back to the days when meat had been a luxury enjoyed only after a matanza, had marked them both with a similar stigmata. 'Señora Monserrat?'

She nodded.

He introduced himself and then, to overcome her nervousness on learning he was a detective, chatted to her about matters that interested them both: the growing lack of water even in wells which in the old days had never once dried up, the ridiculous regulations which laid it down that in street markets cheese could no longer be sold alongside vegetables . . . Soon she was completely at ease and she asked him in for a coffee and brandy.

He introduced the subject of the murder after she'd made the coffee and poured him out a large brandy. 'What was the señor really like?'

She settled on a high stool, added sugar to her mug of coffee. She spoke about Roig, often having trouble in finding the words to express exactly what she wanted to say but, with his sympathetic help, always managing to make it clear what she really meant. Roig had been a man who seemingly could never forget or forgive. When she'd been young, her family had been better off than his—by today's standards, of course, both families had been living in poverty and it would now be difficult to identify any meaningful difference —and this was why, when he'd bought Casa Gran, he'd made a point of searching her out so that he could employ her as his servant and thereby revenge himself . . .

Most men were, as every woman knew, ready to betray their marriages if given half a chance, but normally they did so with as much decorum as possible. But he had betrayed his time and again and never once tried to conceal the fact—in a hazy way, she'd wondered if this was just another expression of his contempt for her. Neither had he hidden the emotionally brutal way in which he'd dismissed each woman in turn when he became bored with her. Why such a succession? What could one woman offer that the previous had not? The only possible answer seemed to be the novelty of a fresh conquest. And while that was perverted enough even when the woman involved had seen more of life than a respectable woman could have done, when his disgusting appetite led him on viciously to corrupt inno- cence . . . She came to a stop, now quite unable to express her feelings.

Alvarez spoke with, apparently, no more than a lazy, casual interest. 'I've had a chat with Señorita Raquel Oliver—I don't know that I'd call her particularly innocent.'

'Another whore,' she said contemptuously.

'Then why d'you talk about him corrupting innocence?'

She did not answer.

'Was one woman different?'

She finished her coffee.

'There was one, wasn't there? Then I need to talk with

her. She will be able to tell me more about him because she
will have loved him, not his cheque-book.'

'What does it matter?'

'He was murdered, señora.'

'He deserved to die.'

'The man who came that afternoon in the white Seat 127
has also been murdered. He didn't deserve such a fate.'

'She'd never kill anyone.'

'I wouldn't suggest for one moment that she might.'

She looked uncertainly at him.

'Señora, this woman who loved him may have learned
something that will tell me why he was murdered and when
I can be certain of the motive, then I will be closer to knowing
who was the murderer.' He spoke even more earnestly so
that it was impossible to miss his sincerity. 'She has no
reason to fear speaking to me. When I have heard what she
can tell me, it will be the end. No one but she and you need
ever know we've met because of him . . . Who is she?' He
waited, knowing that a wrong word now would ensure that
she'd decide to remain silent whereupon nothing, certainly
nothing he could say or do, would ever make her talk.

She spoke slowly, again searching for words. Eulalia had
come from Bodón, on the southern slopes of the Sierra
Nevada on the mainland. The village was perched above a
valley in which the land which could be tilled was of poor
quality and the rest which couldn't—either because of out-
crops of rock or the degree of slope—would support only
goats. The climate was unusually harsh. Due to the shape
and formation of the encircling mountains, the valley was
searingly hot for much of the year; occasionally there were
storms so fierce that the rain flushed the growing crops out
of the ground. The best land—best only in the sense that it
was better than the worst—was almost all owned by absen-
tee landlords who still demanded a full fifty per cent share
from those who sharecropped it. Without any form of indus-
try, very few could hope to work at anything but farming,

however poor the returns that this offered. There was no outright poverty, but there was considerable hardship. A priest came once a fortnight from ten kilometres away and often castigated them for not repairing the church; but how were they to afford even the smallest repair? There was one bar, in which was the only telephone available to the ordinary villagers, one general store which charged too much for everything, one poorly stocked chemist, one baker, and one hardware store.

Life on a tourist island was so different from life on Bodón that it might have been taking place in a different world. Years ago, the people would have heard stories of what life was like on Mallorca, but they would not really have believed them; fairytales were for those who could afford to believe in fairies. But television had changed everything. Now they could see with their own eyes how the farmers on the island grew as many as three crops a year, lived in grand houses, and drove shiny new cars. Their own hardships became much greater because of the comparison.

Eulalia came from a family of nine children, all girls. Her father had demanded a son and had insisted on his wife having child after child in the hopes that the next one would be male (not, however, that any modern and efficient form of contraception would have been open to her even if she had borne a son early on). After the ninth daughter, he had been killed in a rock fall. Her mother (incredibly, remembering all those children) was still fit and strong and she might well have married again had the custom not been that a widower might remarry, but a widow might not. As it was, she was left to try to wrest a living from the poor land which they sharecropped. Hard times became harder. Eulalia, the eldest daughter, had decided to leave Bodón, find work on the island of flowing milk and honey which they'd seen on television, and send money back home.

She'd come to Mallorca and after a short while (short in terms of actual days, not as she at the time and in her nervousness had measured it) had found work as a chamber-maid in one of the hotels on the outskirts of Palma Nova. In the following days, she'd discovered more about life than in all the preceding years. She learned that foreigners had so much money they drank all day long, careless of what excesses they then committed, and knew nothing of the prideful respect for others which came instinctively to any Spaniard; that foreign men considered every female an easy lay and they had not the slightest idea how shocked and humiliated she felt when their hands reached for her breasts and buttocks; and that foreign women expected to be laid, preferably by a Spanish waiter who confided that in reality he was a bullfighter, temporarily down on his luck . . . And yet, despite everything, she did not lose her conviction that good always eventually overcame evil. It was this naïvety which had initially attracted Roig; that, and her innocence.

On first meeting Eulalia, Julia had known that here was an innocent, totally different from all the others, who had no conception of the true nature of Roig and who was making the terrible mistake of believing everything he said.

She'd tried again and again to make Eulalia open her eyes and her heart to the truth, but to no avail. Proudly, Eulalia had refuted all the allegations. Yes, of course Roig had told her he was married, but he'd also explained that he'd never loved his wife and had married her only out of a mistaken sense of compassion. How many men had that nobility of soul? Now his wife was ill, with a complaint that could only be fatal, and after she had died and a decent period of time had passed, he'd marry Eulalia and give her all the things of which until now life had so unfairly deprived her. She'd be able to send enough money back to her family to make their lives easy; she'd have fine clothes and beautiful jewellery; she'd have servants; never again would she have to wonder where the next peseta was coming from . . . A woman of any experience would have laughed in his face at such a shopsoiled approach, but she'd been so naïve that she'd believed every word. So when he pleaded with her to prove that her love for him was as great as his for hers, she'd surrendered her virginity in a mood of exalted pleasure which owed little to plain passion . . .

'Is there such a fool as a woman in love?' she demanded bitterly.

Only a man in love, he thought. 'What ended things between them?'

She got up from the stool and went over to the stove, came back with the coffee maker and refilled their mugs. She passed him the bottle of brandy before settling back on the stool. 'He got bored with her.'

'Because she was no longer innocent?'

She shrugged her shoulders.

'Had she been living in this house?'

'He never lets any of them actually live here. She hasn't a car or anything, so he used to bring her and take her back.'

'Which hotel does she work in?'

'I . . . I don't know.'

'You do, because you'll have kept in touch to try to help her get over what's happened.'

She added brandy to her coffee.

'What's the name of the hotel?'

She drank. For a moment it seemed she was going to continue to refuse to answer, but she then suddenly said: 'The Bahia.'

'I won't forget my promise. No one at the hotel will know why I've spoken to her.'

Fifteen minutes later, he left and returned to his car. He was driving along the dirt track when he saw a man working in the right-hand field and he stopped. He left the car, climbed over the low drystone wall, skirted a large area of melons, and came up to the man who was using a mattock to hoe between the rows of staked beans. 'Ignacio Ferriol?'

Ferriol straightened up.

'My name's Inspector Alvarez, cuerpo general de policia. Have you time for a word?'

'I can make it.'

'Then let's get into some shade.'

They walked across to an algarroba tree and sat.

Alvarez said: 'You told Inspector Jaume that you left here before the white Seat 127 did—is that right?'

'Yes.'

Jaume had also noted, in his meticulously neat handwriting, that Ferriol's manner had suggested he'd been lying, but Jaume had not then pressed the matter because of lack of time. 'Then you've no idea when it drove away?'

'Couldn't have, could I?'

'Couldn't you?'

They were silent. From close by, a couple of cicadas began to shrill, the notes reaching an intensity so piercing that the ear-drums of the two men momentarily vibrated.

'Are you quite certain you didn't see the car leave?' Alvarez persisted.

Ferriol cleared his throat, spat. 'Maybe.'

'What's that mean?'

'I did see a car come away.'

'Was it the white Seat 127?'

'Can't say.'

'Why not?'

'It were dark.'

'You don't live close to here, so what were you doing around at that time?'

'I was . . .' He stopped.

'Well?'

'Picking some beans and tomatoes.'

'Do I look so stupid I might believe that?'

'I tell you, it's bloody true.'

'Then you pick 'em in the dark because they're better flavoured?'

'I picked 'em in the dark because then the old bastard couldn't see me.'

'Ah!' said Alvarez.

Having made the initial admission, Ferriol found it easier to continue. He worked day in, day out, for a man who'd started life the same as everyone else, yet who now strutted about the place as if he'd that moment come down from heaven. And just because he had money, he treated people like Julia and himself as dirt, always criticizing and complaining. One day—last year, it was—he'd come along in his big car just as Ferriol was cycling home. He'd demanded to know what was in the sack balanced on the handlebars. When he'd discovered that it contained newly dug potatoes, he'd threatened to call the police. Stupid bastard. Everyone knew that it was customary for anyone who grew vegetables for someone else to help himself for his own use. And Roig could have afforded to buy whole mountains of potatoes . . .

'So you nipped along after it was dark and while you were busy you saw a car leave Casa Gran—but being dark, you couldn't make out whether it was the same one you'd seen earlier?'

Ferriol nodded.

'Didn't you even get an idea of its colour?'

'I weren't really looking.'

Alvarez pictured the scene. The car's headlights sweeping across the field at each turn or bend in the track, Ferriol crouching low so that he would not be sighted . . . 'Can you tell me anything at all about the car? You must have stood up after it was past and watched it carry on.'

'Nothing to tell except one of its rear lights wasn't working.'

'Which one?'

'I reckon it was the right-hand.'

'What time was this?'

Ferriol considered the question and then muttered to

himself as he worked out the answer. 'Near enough eleven,' he concluded.

If that had been the Seat, thought Alvarez, then it had driven away from Casa Gran inside the period in which, according to the medical evidence, the murder had been committed. 'Was there any other traffic around at the time?'

'Can't say.'

'Why not?'

'Because I wasn't waiting around, that's why not.'

'You'd have heard vehicles and seen their lights.'

'Of course there was cars.'

'On the dirt track leading up to Casa Gran?'

'On the road. There weren't nothing on the track. I said there wasn't.'

Somewhat confusing and contradictory, thought Alvarez, but there seemed no point in pursuing the matter. He changed the conversation. 'I suppose you remember Eulalia?'

'And if I does?'

'How did you find her?'

'Different from the others.'

'Were you surprised to see a woman of her character with Roig?'

'It were a bleeding shame.'

The lightest of breezes just stirred the air and the leaves of the algarobba, but not the clusters of its beans, shivered.

'Did Roig have many visitors apart from the women?'

'He wasn't interested in no one else.'

'Does that mean you didn't see any other visitors here recently—say in the last couple of months?'

Ferriol scratched his wiry, crinkly hair which had turned grey. 'I reckon I've only seen one.'

'Who was that?'

He shrugged his shoulders. 'A boy on a Vespa—don't know who he was.'

'When you say boy, how old d'you mean?'

'Rising twenty.'

'Can you be certain he was visiting Roig and not Julia?'

'If he were, why'd he ask if this was the house where Señor Roig lived? And why, when he came back and I asked him if he'd found the señor, did he reply he had seen that pig of a man?'

'He said, "pig of a man"?'

'It's what I've just said, isn't it?'

'Have you any idea why he talked like that?'

'Why not, since it were true?'

'Can you tell me anything more about this young man?'

'Only that he were an Andaluce.'

'How d'you know that?'

'Where else does a man come from when he swallows half his words and is dressed like a peasant but acts like a duke?'

Alvarez stared across the field at several rows of aubergines. Was there any significance in the fact that Eulalia had also come from Andalucia?

CHAPTER 13

The Hotel Bahia stood back in Palma Nova, at the very limits of a travel agent's within-easy-reach-of-the-sea description. True, because it stood on rising land, the sea was visible from the third floor up, but to reach the beach entailed a ten-minute walk along hot, dusty pavements and across busy roads. Occasionally, the beach was not too crowded for comfort.

It was a hotel which unashamedly catered for the lower end of the market and a holiday there cost almost half what it would much closer to the sea. Standards were of necessity pedestrian; bedrooms were small and the furniture plastic; meals, served buffet style, were invariably unadventurous, an economy which suited most guests, who would have viewed a zarzuela de mariscos with the gravest suspicion; the wine list was limited and the wine waiter ignorant; the discothèque was poorly soundproofed, a fact to which anyone on the first three floors would willingly testify; the water in the swimming pool often took on a green tinge because the filter unit needed replacing.

The assistant manager was relieved when Alvarez made it clear that Eulalia Garcia was not in any sort of trouble. 'I'm glad of that, Inspector.'

'You like her?'

'Yes, I do; but don't get any wrong ideas from that. I just like her in a perfectly straightforward sense, which is why I've helped her when I can.'

'Helped her in what way?'

'To keep on her feet, if you know what I mean? She's so inexperienced, she needs someone advising her. The thing is, she comes from a village on the Peninsula where life is totally different from here; more like it was for us years and years ago. She was telling me that novios still never go out unchaperoned after dark.'

'Try to get our youngsters to behave like that and you'd have a riot on your hands.'

'That's right.'

Yet in Bodón, Alvarez thought, while the decencies might still be observed, life was harsh. 'Could I have a word with her now?'

'Sure. And I expect you'd like to be on your own?'

'If you don't mind.'

The assistant manager stood. 'Inspector . . .' He paused. 'I know you said she wasn't in any trouble, but if she still needs any sort of help and I can give it, call on me.'

'I certainly will.'

After the assistant manager had left, Alvarez went over to the window and, since this office was on the second floor, looked out at other buildings. Years ago, he had known this land when it had been fields, stone walls, trees, and the occasional house or casita; there had been sheep, pigs, mules, chickens, ducks . . . Kestrels had hovered overhead, hoopoes had made their brief, undulating flights, and in May the strikingly coloured bee-eaters had arrived . . . He turned as the door opened.

Eulalia entered the room. 'You wanted to speak to me?' she asked nervously.

He studied her. Quietly attractive in an unsophisticated manner, she was the girl next-door of many years ago. Black hair, an oval face with dark, smooth complexion, deep brown eyes, a shapely nose, a generous mouth, and no make-up. She wore a pink and white apron over blouse and jeans; he was certain she would have felt more comfortable in a frock, but experience with the guests would have taught her that she was safer in the jeans. 'Please come in and sit down, señorita.'

She sat, her hands clasped together and folded in her lap.

'I expect the assistant manager told you I wanted to have a bit of a chat and that's all? I'm investigating the death of Señor Roig.'

She suddenly began to cry and he cursed himself for such blundering insensitivity—but he had assumed that Roig's brutal rejection of her must have destroyed all her love for him. He said apologetically: 'Señorita, please forgive me, but I have to talk about what happened.'

She unclasped her fingers and used her right hand to brush the tears away from her cheeks. 'I'm . . . I'm all right.'

'Let me first assure you of something. What you tell me will be in the strictest confidence.' With sudden anger, he thought of Roig, perversely drawn by her innocence, setting out to destroy it because if he succeeded then his pleasure would be all the greater. His anger was replaced by renewed sympathy for her. He tried to find words that could offer some comfort. 'Señorita, from my own experience I can assure you that even the most terrible sadness is softened by time.'

She shook her head, denying the possibility.

'A family can provide a support that no one else can, so why not return home?'

'I can't.'

'Why not?'

'I . . . I have to make money and send it back to them.'

'I promise you, money can never be that important.'

She remained silent.

He sighed. Roig had promised her money which she could send home, correctly judging that to do so would make her seduction easier; now, she was seeing the sacrifice of the love and the comfort of her family as a price she must pay for her sin.

She suddenly said, with desperate intensity: 'I didn't kill him.'

'Señorita, not for one second have I ever thought such a thing possible. My only reason for being here now is to find out if perhaps you know something which will help me identify who did kill him.'

She shook her head.

'You may believe you do not, but not recognize the meaning of what you do know. Tell me, can you think of anyone who didn't like him?'

She spoke haltingly and it soon became clear she really knew so little beyond the false, romantic image she had sought that she was not going to be able to help. Then, after she'd answered several questions, she began to speak of the past—as if, he thought, she was trying to learn how she could have acted as she had. In Bodón, no respectable girl was ever alone with a boy unless he was her novio and even then never after dark. This, naturally, did not prevent sidelong glances which spoke volumes; and even, so it was said, if a girl were really fast, with assignations. But she had never given encouragement to any boy. She gained comfort from conforming to the conventions. And up to the day she had left Bodón, no boy had declared himself to her mother,

perhaps because she was one of nine and therefore could
bring little to her marriage . . .

Life on Mallorca had bewildered and at times frightened
her. But the staff of the hotel had been kind and she'd
learned not to be too shocked by what she saw and she'd
sent as much money as possible home. The letters from
there—written by her eldest sister since her mother could
not read or write—told her what a difference the money
made and that had pleased her, but they'd also made her
very homesick . . .

Initially, she'd been bewildered by Roig's attentions. He
was so rich, he made no secret of the fact he was married,
and he was more than twice her age. She'd expressed her
bewilderment to one of the other chambermaids, who'd
laughed and called her a real innocent . . .

Roig had seduced her by all the means Julia had already
described to Alvarez. Later, a whole life later, there'd been
the morning when he'd curtly told her that it would be best
if they parted.

'Señorita, did you see him again?'

'No,' she whispered.

'But I expect you tried to speak to him?'

'I couldn't understand . . . I couldn't believe he'd
just . . .'

'Did you telephone him?'

She nodded.

'What happened?'

'Julia told me he was there, at Casa Gran and she'd get
him, but when she came back to the phone she said he'd
just left. Then I tried his office, but the secretary said he
wasn't in. It was the same every time I tried.'

'Did you ever return to Casa Gran to try and meet him
face-to-face?'

'I couldn't.'

Had she gone, she might have met her successor. Alvarez
fiddled with his lower lip for a few seconds, then said:

'Señorita, do you know anyone on this island who also comes from Andalucia?'

She looked at him in surprise; she nodded.

'Who is he?'

'Carlos Vidal.'

'Whereabouts does he come from?'

'Posuna.'

'Is that near Bodón?'

'Yes.'

'Did you know him before you came here?'

'Yes.'

'Perhaps you came because he was already here?'

Her brief reserve came to an end and she once more spoke freely. Vidal had left Posuna many months before, determined to find a better life than any local village could offer. His letters home had astonished everyone with their accounts of wealth beyond normal imagination; wealth even greater than the television had ever shown. Fired by his stories, she had come to Mallorca, seeking the pot of gold at the end of the rainbow . . .

'Is he your novio?'

'I told you, I haven't a novio.'

'Even so, I imagine you've seen a lot of him?'

'It's difficult. He works in a hotel in Porto Cristo.'

'But surely he can get around easily enough on his Vespa?'

She failed to be surprised by his knowledge that Vidal owned a Vespa. 'He came here once or twice and we'd talk about home, but then . . .' She tailed off into silence.

'He ceased coming to see you?'

She nodded.

'Was that because of Roig?'

'He wouldn't understand,' she said, bitter for the first time. 'I kept explaining that Pablo's marriage wasn't a real one . . .' She stopped. His marriage had proved to be more durable than his affair with her.

'Did you see him at all after you'd become friendly with Roig?'

'Only once.'

'What happened?'

'He . . . he was horrible.'

He tried to place the relationship between them, but couldn't. Vidal was not her novio and had their previous acquaintanceship warmed into real friendship, then surely he would have seen as much as possible of her—a Vespa would not take all that long to get from Porto Cristo to Palma Nova? Against that, he had obviously been outraged by her affair with Roig and this suggested jilted and jealous love. A man was seldom outraged by another man's seduction unless himself emotionally involved. And why had he travelled to Casa Gran, when he knew she would not be there; why had he referred to Roig in such contemptuous terms, when speaking to Ferriol, if not jealous? . . .

'Señorita, thank you for helping me. Please think very seriously about returning to your family.' He saw from the way her mouth tightened that, sadly, she had no intention of doing so.

CHAPTER 14

Alvarez parked in front of Braddon's house, climbed out of the car and walked towards the front door and this, for a brief moment, brought him in sight of the swimming pool; Braddon was sitting out on the pool patio, his look of sullen dissatisfaction obvious even at that distance. Alvarez walked on. Only those with practical experience knew what hell a lotus existence could become to someone psychologically unsuited to its style of freedom. Impotent bitterness was a potent fuel, especially to a man with a quick temper . . .

The maid opened the front door and he was explaining

to her what he wanted when Letitia entered the hall from the sitting-room. 'It's you!' she said sharply.

'Señora, I must apologize for disturbing you, but I have to ask your husband some questions.'

'You've asked him more than enough already.' She stared belligerently at him. 'Haven't you yet found out who killed Roig?'

'I am afraid not.'

'He was a crook.'

'Perhaps regrettably, that was not sufficient justification for killing him.'

'You're entitled to your opinion, I'm entitled to mine . . . Well, I suppose you'd better come on through.'

He followed her into the sitting-room and then out on to the pool patio. Braddon was wearing only shorts and his chest was nearly the colour of bronze.

Letitia said: 'He wants to ask you more questions. God knows why. If he can't judge you're incapable of killing anyone, he's not much of a detective.' It was impossible to judge whether she had momentarily forgotten that Alvarez spoke fluent English or was being deliberately rude.

Braddon, who had not come to his feet, looked up, squinting because of the sun. 'I told you last time, I had a bit of a row with him, but that's all. And what I'd like to know is, who wouldn't in the circumstances?'

'Very few, señor.'

He was surprised by such an answer and it was several seconds before he said: 'Then why go on and on about things?'

'Because he was murdered.'

'But it wasn't anything to do with me.'

'Yet surely you wish to help me discover who it was who killed him?'

'Why the hell should I care? Bloody good luck to whoever it was. I'll tell you, it's no good looking to me for crocodile tears; I never did believe in that nonsense about forgetting

what a bloke was really like just as soon as he's dead. Roig
was a pure corkscrew of a bastard . . .'

She hurriedly interrupted him. 'Joe, don't let yourself get
so worked up.'

'What d'you expect me to do, knowing he swindled me
and what that means to us? If I had the chance—'

She interrupted him again, before he could finish whatever he'd been going to say, and she decided it would be
politic to swallow her true feelings and offer Alvarez a more
friendly welcome. 'Why are we still standing?'

'I'm not,' observed Braddon.

'Inspector, do sit down; I think you'll find that chair there
will be the most comfortable.'

He sat on the wood and canvas chair which was partially
within the shade of the sun umbrella set in a concrete base.

'Well, what is it this time?' demanded Braddon, accepting
that he'd have to cooperate, at least to some degree.

'Señor, since speaking to you on Sunday, I've learned
certain things and you may be able to help me interpret
them and find out what they really mean.'

Letitia moved a chair and sat close to her husband, ready
to try to cut short any further rashness on his part.

'Señor Roig knew an Englishman, Señor Oakley. Have
you met Señor Oakley?'

'No,' replied Braddon.

'He had a house in Llueso.'

'It doesn't alter anything if he had a house in Timbuktu.
I've never met him.'

Letitia put a hand on his forearm, but he shrugged it off.

'He also has been murdered.'

'So are you going to be daft enough to suggest I killed
him as well?'

'How terrible!' she said, trying to counter the suggestion
of indifference to another murder—which, she was certain,
might be interpreted as a mask to other and deeper emotions
—which her husband's manner had given.

'He was murdered for one of two reasons. Either he knew who killed Roig and therefore had to be silenced, or it was because he and Roig had done business together. At the moment, I think the latter possibility is the more likely . . . Señor, do you know the name of Andreu y Soler?'

'Never heard of it.'

'They are developing the urbanización of La Portaña.'

'Never heard of that either.'

'Yes, you have, Joe,' she said.

'When I say I haven't, I mean I bloody well haven't.'

'But we went to have a look at it only last month . . .'

'No, we didn't.'

'That's the place you'd read about and couldn't understand why everything was so terribly expensive and you wanted to see it for yourself. And when you saw it, you said it was just for catching people who are snobs. And afterwards we went to the Chinese restaurant . . .'

'I tell you, I've never seen the bloody place.'

She belatedly realized that if she continued to insist that he had, she would either make herself look stupid or her husband a liar. 'No, you're right. I've just remembered, it's John I went with because you weren't feeling well. And he didn't like Chinese food, but was too polite to tell me beforehand because I'd said I loved it. And when he didn't finish his spring rolls . . .' She came to a stop, realizing that she was sounding less and less convincing.

Alvarez said: 'Señor, have you heard of a firm, registered in the Cayman Islands, called Ashley Developments?'

'No.'

'Then now I have asked all the questions.' He stood. 'Except there is one more. Have you been able to remember someone who can vouch for the fact that on the night of the eighth you did not leave this house?'

'I've already told you,' she said, her tone now once more sharp, 'I was here and he never moved.'

'But have you managed to remember someone else?'

'No,' said Braddon pugnaciously, 'but that doesn't alter anything. I was bloody here and you can try as hard as you like and you won't prove differently.'

Hotel Rocador was just over a kilometre outside Porto Cristo and the natural harbour which made the port a haven for yachtsmen. Situated on top of a cliff, it had a superb view out to sea. It was family owned, and even though virtually all the guests came on package holidays, they were treated with respect and attention, with the result that many of them came year after year.

The receptionist said that Vidal was off duty and suggested he might be in his digs in Porto Cristo. Alvarez drove back to the port. Camino S'on Perragut, at the western end, wound up a hill to a dead-end at the top. No. 41 was the last house on the right, remarkable for the shade of violet in which the shutters had been painted.

An elderly woman led him through the house and into a small enclosed patio. She pointed to the two-floor building on the far side and said that Vidal lived in the bedroom on the top floor.

He climbed the wooden stairs, past three cages containing canaries, and reached a small landing. From the room came the clash of rock music. He knocked on the door, but was hardly surprised when there was no response. He opened the door and stepped inside. Vidal, wearing only boxer shorts, was lying on the bed; he had been reading a magazine. 'What d'you want?' he shouted.

'Silence, to begin with.'

He hesitated, then leaned over and switched off the tape-recorder.

'Cuerpo general de policia.' He was not surprised to see the wary, defensive response to this announcement; most people, even those who lived lives whiter than new-fallen snow, reacted initially in the same way. 'Mind if I sit?'

Vidal came to his feet in one swift, graceful movement,

crossed to the only chair, picked up a pile of magazines and dropped them on to the floor, gestured with his right hand. 'For you, señor.'

Mockery, or extravagant courtesy? You never knew with an Andaluce, thought Alvarez. He sat and the chair creaked, making him wonder if it would collapse since it was obviously riddled with worm holes. 'I'm making inquiries into the murder of Pablo Roig—you'll have heard about it?'

'Someone at the hotel did mention it.'

'You don't sound very concerned. But surely you knew him?'

'On the contrary.'

'Are you saying that you never met him?'

'No. Merely that I did not know him.'

'So you'd agree that you saw him at his house, Casa Gran?'

Vidal inclined his head.

'When?'

'Perhaps a month ago.'

'Do you know Señorita Garcia, or have you merely met her?'

If Vidal resented the form of the question, he did not show this. 'I know her.'

'Is this from some time back?'

'It is from when we were both young.'

'How would you describe the relationship between the two of you?'

'To a stranger, I would not.'

'Then think of me as a friend. Are you fond of her?'

'Naturally.'

'Were you in love with her before she met Roig?'

He said, with haughty scorn: 'That is a ridiculous question.'

For once, Alvarez's normally equable temper rose. This young man could now think of her only as damaged goods and a noble Andaluce demanded a woman of purity since only then could she be good enough to be his wife. 'D'you mind getting off your high horse and telling me just why it's so ridiculous?'

He looked at Alvarez, surprised but not alarmed, by the harshness with which the question had been put. 'Because she is my second cousin.'

Alvarez had seldom felt such a fool.

'Our great-grandparents lived in Bodón and my grand-mother married a man from Posuna. They didn't welcome the marriage since the people of Bodón have always regarded themselves as superior to those of Posuna. That is ridiculous, of course.'

'You seem to a find that a lot in this world is ridiculous.'

'I do.'

It was only coincidence that Vidal had been looking directly at him as he spoke, Alvarez assured himself. 'Let's get back to Roig. You went to Casa Gran and saw him there, didn't you?'

'Did I?'

'You've forgotten that Señora Monserrat let you into the house and took you out to the courtyard where he was?'

He did not answer.

'What happened then?'

'He was insolent.'

'Which infuriated you?'

'Did it?'

'Did you visit the place again?'

'Perhaps.'

'To speak to him about what?'

'To explain what he must do.'

'Which was?'

'The matter is no concern of yours.'

'On the contrary; I'm investigating his murder.'

'My visit had nothing to do with that.'

'I'll be the judge.'

He was silent.

'Who was in the house this second time?'

'Roig and a woman.'

'Who was she?'

'A whore.'

'How can you be so certain?'

'I am neither blind nor deaf,' he said scornfully.

'Did you speak to him?'

'I tried.'

'What's that mean?'

'He refused to listen to what I had to say or to promise to do what I asked him to do.'

'Did he admit to having known Señorita Garcia?'

'He merely called me a naïve bumpkin who knew nothing about the world. The whore laughed.'

'So what did you do or say?'

'I left.'

'But not before having one hell of a row?'

'No.'

'You want me to believe that you didn't tell him what you thought of him and his previous ten generations? With all your overdeveloped pride, you didn't threaten to push his head through his fundament for treating you like that in front of a woman?'

'One does not demean oneself by arguing with a peasant.'

Reluctantly, Alvarez had to admire the spirit of a man who, himself poor, could mean it when he referred to an extremely rich man as a peasant. 'When did you next visit Casa Gran?'

'I didn't.'

'Weren't you there on the night of the eighth?'

'If I didn't return, I can't have been.'

'Surely you wanted to revenge yourself on someone who'd insulted your pride and made a woman laugh at you, even if you weren't prepared to argue with him?'

'A man can only be insulted by his equals or his betters.'

'Then you seldom feel insulted?'

He disdained to answer.

'Can you prove where you were on the night of the eighth?'
He shrugged his shoulders.

'I advise you at least to try.'

He thought for quite a time. 'I came off duty at seven.'

'So what did you do after then?'

'I probably came back here; perhaps after having a drink at a bar.'

'Is there anyone who can vouch for seeing you during the evening?'

'Why should they bother?'

'To prove you're telling the truth when you say you didn't go to Casa Gran.'

'I do not lie.'

If he'd been wearing a sword, thought Alvarez, he'd have touched the hilt with an unmistakable gesture. Andalucia now had an autonomous government. It was a pity they had not seen fit to ban emigration.

Alvarez arrived downstairs the following morning at nine o'clock and Dolores called out from the front room, where she had been polishing the furniture, that she had been out while he had been snoring and had bought him a couple of ensaimadas; they were on the kitchen table and for his chocolate all he had to do was put a light under the saucepan and warm it up. Admirable woman, he thought, as he lit the gas. He sat at the table and ate the ensaimadas with butter and apricot jam and drank two cupfuls of hot chocolate. An excellent way of starting the day—perhaps a slightly late start, as he was reminded when the clock in the dining-room chimed the half-hour. In view of this fact, it seemed wiser not to go straight to the post, but to do something which could reasonably be brought forward as a valid excuse for not having been in the office at eight, if challenged on that point. What? Now that he knew that any specific reference either to Andreu y Soler or Ashley Developments was important, surely a second and much more careful examination of all the papers in Oakley's house was necessary?

He drove out of Llueso on to the Puerto Llueso road and down that to the dirt track which gave access to Ca'n Tardich. The house and its setting were looking exceedingly attractive in the morning sunshine and as he left the car he experienced a rare sense of optimism. Perhaps luck was finally about to reward him and he'd be able to buy a property such as this one? Happy the man who, before he died, could run his fingers through rich soil and know it was his . . .

Beatriz opened the front door.

''Morning,' he said, with unusual cheerfulness. 'I've just come along to have another look through the house.'

'I don't know about that,' she answered uncertainly. 'With the señor back, I don't think I ought to let you in without him saying it's all right and he's out at the moment.'

CHAPTER 15

'What?' shouted Salas.

Alvarez stared gloomily at the top of his desk. 'It seems, señor, that he is, after all, alive.'

There was a very long pause. 'I just do not believe this can be happening to me.'

'I haven't had a chance to question him yet, because he was out when I went to his house. But the maid says that he's reported his car as stolen from the airport car park, so perhaps we ought to tell Traffic . . .'

'How long is it since you assured me he had been murdered?'

'I know, only . . .'

'Yet now you tell me he has not been murdered.'

'Señor, it has been very difficult. If you could look at things from my point of view . . .'

'Only by standing on my head.'

'All the evidence did point to the fact . . .'

'You're surely not suggesting that at any time in this case you have bothered about anything so mundane as the evidence?'

'Señor . . .'

'First you tell me he is a suspect in the murder of Roig.'

'Yes, but . . .'

'And without once pausing to make certain you have considered all the relevant facts, you contact England and ask them to conduct a search for him.'

'That's not exactly right. It was you who . . .'

'Having done that, you decided he had not murdered Roig and fled the island, but had been murdered. So you had to get in touch with England and admit your mistake, making everyone here, and in particular yourself, look foolish. But that's not the end of the matter. Things had become confused by most people's standards, but not by yours and you are only happy when surrounded by total confusion. So you now announce to me that he wasn't murdered, he's alive and well. Which means you're going to have to ring England yet again and explain that the man you said was alive, then dead, is alive again . . .'

Alvarez reached down with his free hand and pulled open the bottom right-hand drawer of the desk. To his consternation, he saw that it contained only a glass and a couple of dusty files. He'd forgotten to replace the bottle of brandy.

He parked on one side of the gnarled olive tree in front of Ca'n Tardich; on the other side was a Seat Panda, it's right-hand rear window displaying the forms which marked it as a hire car. He crossed to the front door and rang the bell.

Oakley was taller than he, but considerably thinner—a man who either exercised regularly or took care not to eat

too generously. He had a round face, with eyes set high, full
cheeks, and a generous mouth that looked as if about to
break into a grin; his hair was a medium brown, held a very
slight curl at the front, and was clearly thinning on top. He
wore a safari shirt and cotton trousers, both well pressed,
and his leather sandals were well polished. 'Good morning,'
he said in Spanish.

Alvarez introduced himself in English.

Oakley smiled. 'Then this must be the quickest slice of
action the island's ever seen!'

'I'm sorry, señor, I don't understand.'

'It's no time at all since I reported my car had been stolen
from the airport.'

'I haven't come about that.'

'Not?'

'Your car is in Palma, with the Traffic department. It is
quite undamaged and was never stolen. I ordered Traffic to
drive it from the airport to their workshops to examine it.'

'Why on earth do that?'

'Hasn't Beatriz explained to you what has been happening?'

'She did try to tell me something after she'd got over
treating me as a ghost, but I was in a hurry so I'm afraid I
cut her short. So what's been going on which seems to have
excited so many people?'

'We believed you to be dead.'

'I'm happy to echo Twain and say that the reports were
exaggerated . . . Why did anyone think that?'

'It's quite a long story.'

'Then let's go through and sit and have a drink while you
tell it; I find that long stories heard standing up and dry
tend to become tedious.'

They went through the house and out on to the vine-
covered patio. 'What would you like?' asked Oakley. 'I can
offer all the usual drinks, plus one or two minor exotics.'

'May I have a coñac, please, with ice.'

When Oakley returned, he passed one glass across, sat, raised his own. 'The first today, but not the last, if God grants me a fine repast. A toast which suggests a touch of gluttony, but for my money that's by far the least of the deadly sins . . . Now, that long story—edited, perhaps?'

Alvarez gave him a résumé of the facts.

'It seems life on the island isn't as sleepy as I've always assumed it to be. Poor old Pablo!'

'You didn't know he'd been murdered?'

'How could I? I've not read a local paper since the day I left and, with all due respect to Pablo's memory, his death isn't an international event. Obviously, this was what Beatriz was trying to tell me—she rather tends to wallow in disasters.'

'You'll forgive me for saying so, señor, but you don't sound very upset by his murder.'

'I'm surprised, in a sense shocked, but not emotionally upset, if that answers you?'

'Are you saying that you didn't like him?'

'To be honest, I neither liked nor disliked him.'

'Your relationship, then, was purely a business one?'

'That's right. Do you know who murdered him?'

'Not yet.'

'Then presumably you're now trying to decide whether I might have done?'

'I naturally have to examine all possibilities.'

'And, to pin you down, I am a possibility?'

'Señor, until I know all the facts, I have to accept that any one of several people might have killed him.'

'What brings me within this uncharmed circle? Simply the fact that we did business together? I don't think so, because if you included his legal work, that qualification unqualified would provide you with an embarrassment of suspects. When was he murdered?'

'On the night of the eighth.'

'That's Monday of last week, isn't it? The day I went

over and saw him in his country place. So presumably that's the real reason why I've become a suspect?'

'I understand that while you were there, you had a heated row with him?'

'Overheard by his daily? In fact, that's not a strictly accurate description. He became heated, but I remained cool.'

'What was the row about?'

'You will keep everything I tell you confidential?'

'Unless the needs of the case demand otherwise.'

'Is that a polite way of saying, unless you decide to charge me with the murder? Since I didn't kill him, I hope there's no fear of that. I represent an investment company . . .'

'Ashley Developments, registered in the Cayman Islands?'

Oakley whistled. 'You've been doing your homework to some purpose! Yes, that's right. Well, cutting things short, I decided some little time ago that there was still scope for a good investment in an up-market development close to Palma. So we formed a Spanish company to buy the land and appointed Roig as the legal adviser. Between you and me, I knew enough about him to reckon that if anyone could get planning permission, he would. He did. So the development was started and it proved convenient to channel much of the early financing through him.

'Then, things started to go wrong and the banks, who'd been brought in as investors, began to make unpleasant noises. I hurried back here and checked things and found that although costs had risen beyond our estimates—don't they always?—and sales were not as good as we'd forecast, the financial shortfall couldn't be explained unless someone was screwing the company. Some hard lucubration identified who that someone probably was and so I had a chat with Roig and hinted at what I suspected, in the hope that he'd see the advantages to himself of keeping things quiet and so would refund the money.

'He didn't. That meant that eventually I had to get very much tougher. I said I wanted another talk with him and he didn't have any doubts what it would be about. He suggested meeting at his place in the country—presumably because there there was no fear of leaks.

'When I saw him, I gave him all the facts quite bluntly and told him that his connection with the company was over and if he didn't repay every last peseta within two weeks, the facts would be given to the police.'

'What was his reaction?'

'Highly emotional and embarrassing. There's a lot to be said for the English stiff upper lip, even if we're told that the repression of emotions . . . He confessed he was a compulsive gambler. He'd stolen in order to gamble and had lost everything and there was no way in which he could repay within the fortnight. He beseeched me not to tell the police and drew a vivid picture of the utter distress of his wife and daughters if he were sent to prison. He swore on every saint in the calendar—and some that probably aren't —that if I'd give him more time, he'd repay everything. I explained that that was impossible. The banks had given the company a deadline and I was certain they'd stick to it and wouldn't extend credit facilities because word had reached me that another property company reckoned La Portaña would be a very good buy at a reduced price, which the banks could offer after taking possession and adding their own profits on to the deal.'

'How did he react when you told him it was impossible to give him longer than the fortnight?'

'Very scared and acting angry to cover up that fact. He made a lot of silly threats and I laughed at him, which didn't help matters.'

'What kind of threats?'

'If I went to the police, he'd see a friend who'd make certain that I'd wake up suddenly to discover that my head had just parted with my neck.'

'You're saying he threatened to have you killed?'

'He was so scared he didn't know what he was saying.'

Assuming that the facts were true, thought Alvarez, it was wrong contemptuously to dismiss the possibility of violent retribution. Roig had come from the humblest of backgrounds and had believed himself despised because of this. He had worked his way up the ladder of success to reach the top, a very wealthy man who, at least in his own eyes, had become highly respected and envied. Suddenly, he had been threatened with exposure as a common thief. He might well have been ready to take any step to prevent this happening. And as a solicitor, he must have come into contact with men to whom violence was a way of life; men who would accept a contract on anyone at the right price. But what he would not have realized was that in employing such a man he was putting himself at grave risk. To them, loyalty was a meaningless word. If he paid half the agreed price in advance—a normal condition—the would-be assassin might well deem it easier and safer to kill him and settle for that half, rather than to go ahead with the assassination in order to claim the other half . . .

'Have you had a good journey?'

He started. 'I am very sorry, señor; my mind was a long way away.'

Oakley chuckled. 'I'd say, almost in the next galaxy.'

'What did you do when he made this threat?'

'What else was there to do but leave?'

'What was the time then?'

He shrugged his shoulders. 'It was getting on, but I've no real idea.'

'Was it dark?'

'No.'

'Did you come straight back here?'

'That's right. And spent several hours with the company's figures, trying to find a way of preventing the banks foreclosing and getting a bargain.'

'You must have resented what Roig had done?'

'That's too mild a word. But I was almost as angry with myself because I should have kept a much closer watch on the figures and realized what was happening much sooner, when the survival of the company couldn't have been put at risk. The real trouble was, I'd trusted him too much because I'd reckoned that while he'd normally cut any corners he could, he'd never betray his own clients—perhaps on the analogy of the dog and its doorstep.'

'Is there anyone who can verify that you were here, in the house, on the night of the murder?

'No. You've only my word for it that I was . . . And from the look on your face, that is not quite sufficient.'

'Señor, you left here very suddenly and unexpectedly on Tuesday.'

'That's quite right.'

'Why was that?'

'Because during the morning, I decided to chase a source of capital I'd identified, but not yet captured. Since time was all-important, I gathered up all my papers and took off at full speed; there just wasn't the time to make any arrangements, such as leaving Beatriz her money.'

'Did you catch the plane to Heathrow for which you bought a first-class ticket?'

'That's an odd question.'

'Possibly, but I would like an answer.'

'Frankly, I see no joy in paying the exorbitant price of a first-class ticket and then not using it; yes, I did fly.'

'One of the first-class passengers who had booked, failed to turn up.'

'They told me I'd taken the last seat, but I did notice there was an empty one on the flight. That's very usual. You must know as well as I that businessmen on full fare tickets make several bookings and then use the one which best suits them.'

'Do you think the cabin staff will remember you?'

'I rather doubt it, when you think of all the different faces they see every time they fly.'

'Have you any idea why I had your car driven from the airport to Traffic?'

'How could I have?'

'It was to discover whether there were any traces in it which might link you to the murder.'

'Then it was a wasted effort.'

'There were bloodstains on the steering-wheel, back seat, and rubber mat on the back floor.'

'Are you quite sure of that . . . Of course! Just before I set off for the airport, I cut my arm. It didn't look anything, but I bled like a stuck pig for a while.'

'How did it happen?'

'Like most accidents, through carelessness. My suitcase is old and battered and the wire strengthening that runs round the edges has broken through the binding at one or two points. I was manœuvring the case into the back when my foot slipped and I fell against it; the exposed wire had a nick in it and the edge sliced through my shirt and into my flesh. The cut bled so much I had to go back inside for a plaster. When I saw the mess I'd made on the seat and mat I tried to clear up, but being in a rush obviously made a bad job of things.'

'Don't you usually put your luggage in the boot?'

'Not when the back seat's empty; it's a habit of mine that used to annoy my wife. She has a very logical and tidy mind so luggage goes into the boot; my habit of mixing up my socks and my handkerchiefs in the drawer is something else that used to infuriate her.'

'You are still married?'

'I'm not certain. We decided some time back that enough was enough and she may have divorced me by now.'

'Where is your home?'

'This is my home.'

'Beatriz says you are seldom here.'

'Nevertheless, since my marriage broke up, it's the nearest thing to a permanent one that I have.'

'Then where do you live when you're away?'

'Out of a suitcase.'

'Where does your wife live?'

'Frankly, I've not the slightest idea, but there is one thing for sure: wherever it is, she'll be in debt. In twenty years I never managed to teach her that nations could spend beyond their means with impunity, but individuals couldn't . . . Your glass is empty and I'm being a very poor host. Will you have the same again?'

'Thank you. But first, do you know what is your blood group?'

'Off-hand, no, but there's a note of it in my diary, so I can look it up.'

Oakley carried the glasses into the house. He soon returned, sat. 'My blood group is O.'

'Whereabouts did you cut your arm?'

Oakley pulled up the short sleeve of his shirt to show a cut, part of the scab of which had become brushed off. 'Doesn't look good for more than a couple of small drops of blood, does it, but at the time there was a moment when I wondered if I was going to have to get a doctor to stitch it.'

He'd an answer for everything, thought Alvarez. Because he was telling the truth or because he'd thought up the questions first? 'I must ask you for your passport.'

'Why?'

'I will hold it until my investigations are complete.'

'Then although I've explained everything, you now see me as a definite suspect?'

'I would prefer to say, a material witness.'

'Yes, that does sound much better . . . What do I do if I need to leave the island on business?'

'Should that situation arise, señor, if you will get in touch with me I will see what arrangements can be made.'

Oakley raised his glass and drank; his expression

remained bland, as if he saw nothing more than a passing irritation in what had been said.

Alvarez spoke to Traffic and explained that Oakley would be in Palma that afternoon and it was in order to deliver his car to him. 'But right now, would you go and check whether both rear lights are working?'

Several minutes later he was informed: 'The rear right-hand driving one is on the blink.'

CHAPTER 16

Alvarez telephoned the airport and eventually the call was answered; he asked to speak to the cabin staff personnel manager. There was another long wait before he was connected to her office.

'I don't understand,' she said, in her high-pitched and rather arrogant voice.

Patiently, he explained a second time. 'I need to speak to the cabin staff who were on flight IB 628 on Tuesday, the ninth.'

'Yes, yes, but why?'

'To find out if any of them can verify that a certain person was on that flight.'

'It's a very unusual request.'

'It's a very unusual case, señorita.'

'Señora,' she snapped.

Brave man, he thought.

'You obviously have no idea what it is that you're asking. The cabin staff do not necessarily stay together and by now the people in question may be working several planes. How am I supposed to arrange to get them all together?'

'Might they not, perhaps, still all be flying together?'

It was not an admission she was prepared to make.

'If you would be kind enough to arrange things; it is important.'

'Is there anything more?'

He ignored her sarcasm and thanked her for her cooperation.

He made a second call to England and asked to speak to Inspector Mallinson.

There was a short wait before a cheerful voice said: 'Good morning. Rather, it would be here if it weren't raining quite so hard. I suppose it's sunny with you?'

'Too sunny.'

'That is quite impossible . . . Well, how can I help?'

'You will remember why I've been in touch with your department before?'

'Of course; the now-you-see-him-now-you-don't case.'

'I beg your pardon?'

'Sorry, just a little nonsense,' said Mallinson hastily, realizing that his listener might not share the sense of humour. 'As a matter of fact, I was going to call you a bit later on, but let's hear what you have to say first.'

'I've questioned Oakley and he's evasive when it comes to details of his past life and I'm wondering—as I believe someone your side did—whether there's any significance in this. As I now have his passport, I thought the number might help to trace out his background?'

'Undoubtedly. But it might give some information more quickly and directly. As you've probably seen, at the back there are two spaces for names and addresses, to be entered by the holder, of relatives or friends in case of emergencies. Does he give anything away there?'

'Only one of the two spaces has been filled up and that's had a slip of paper pasted over it, as directed in case of change of address, and all that is now listed is his address here. Naturally, I intend to have the laboratory remove the slip and discover what was written originally, but I was hoping you'd start what inquiries you can at your end before that's done?'

'Of course . . . So if you'll give me the number?'

Alvarez read it out.

'Right. Now, I've a request. As soon as we heard from you that Oakley was very much alive, we alerted the Fraud Squad. They're greatly interested and want to know if you can keep him on the island until someone from them can get over to question him?'

'That is no problem. As I have said, I have his passport and I have already warned ports and the airport not to allow him passage out.'

'Couldn't be better . . . It appears that inquiries into the insider dealing case have virtually come to a full stop through lack of any proof; there's just not a tittle of evidence to show the suspect's reaping any benefits he shouldn't and the circumstances being what they are, that's a key necessity. Oakley may well prove to be the missing link.'

'You have not been able to discover anything out about Ashley Developments?'

'Our lawyers have tried all they can and got nowhere. Insider trading is not a criminal offence in the Caymans, so despite all the treaties recently signed between them and us, in this case company and banking secrecy remains inviolate . . . If ever you need to squirrel away a load of money, I recommend there.'

'Unfortunately, I don't think I shall ever have the need.'

Mallinson chuckled. 'It's doubly unjust when you aren't even given the chance of deciding to enjoy the wages of sin, isn't it?'

After the call was finished, Alvarez leaned back in the chair and rested his feet on the desk. Surely the picture was slowly becoming clear? A man in London decided to use inside information to make a fortune on the Stock Exchange. But if he bought shares heavily either in his own name or that of anyone close to him, an investigation would surely disclose what he had done. So he had to create an impenetrable barrier between the information and the reward. In other words, Ashley Developments, owned in whole or part by him, registered in the Cayman Islands, a possession which, lacking any criminal content there, would never be traced to him. Ashley Developments had invested the money in at least one development, perhaps in more—what good was money if not used to make more money? Obviously, such a scheme supposed one potentially dangerous disadvantage: that whoever had actual control of Ashley Developments might abscond with its assets because he knew that no action would ever be brought against him by the man in England since to do so would be for the latter to expose himself to criminal action. This meant that the man in England had to be able to trust absolutely the man abroad—quite a requirement, since in financial matters the degree of honesty shown was usually in inverse proportion to the amount at stake.

Ashley Developments had formed Andreu y Soler in order to develop La Portaña. Property development was a high risk enterprise, but there were still very good profits to be made if one could identify a market that would appeal to new buyers. La Portaña was one such. Unfortunately, success had been slow in coming and the banks, who'd loaned large sums of money, were threatening to foreclose; and their interests seemed to lie in carrying out their threats since another property company was willing to buy the urbanización from them at a price which would give them a handsome profit.

It had been discovered by Oakley that the primary cause of the company's financial problems wasn't simply faulty estimates and poor sales, it was that the company had systematically been swindled by Roig. A truly honest man —which Oakley had to be since he'd been entrusted with the running of Ashley Developments—valued his honesty as perceived in the eyes of others at far above rubies. Yet if

Andreu y Soler collapsed and all the money which had been poured into the urbanización was lost because of the swindle, it might well look to the man in England—since nothing tainted a judgement more quickly than losing a fortune—that Oakley had stolen the money and his attempts to blame someone else marked him out as a coward as well as a swindler. So, knowing that his reputation for honesty was at risk, Oakley had hated Roig; hated him so much that he'd lost control of himself and killed the man who was about to strip him of what he most prized . . .

Julia was in the middle of the field to the side of her casita, bent double, picking beans for the market at Moldia the next morning; in front of the casita, Adolfo Monserrat, her son, sat drinking. He watched Alvarez approach, then said in a surly tone: 'Something you want?'

'I'd like to speak to your mother.'

'Why?'

'I'll explain to her, not you.'

'Who the bleeding hell d'you think you are, coming here and talking like that?'

'Cuerpo general de policia,' replied Alvarez. He walked from the dirt-floored patio to the field. She turned her head and saw him approach, but did not straighten up until she had finished picking the beans off a plant. There were lines of tiredness in her face, highlighted by the shadow thrown by the broad-rimmed raffia hat she wore. People in towns were forever moaning about the price of vegetables, he thought, but put them to work producing them and then no price would be high enough.

'Good afternoon, señora. I need a word, but there's no hurry; I don't want to interrupt your work.'

'I've nearly finished.'

'Let me help.'

The offer flustered her. She said that perhaps she'd enough already, since the bean crop was peaking and so would everyone else's be and maybe not all the ones she had already picked would be sold . . .

He began to pick the beans. The sun drew the sweat out of him and in no time at all his back and legs ached and his belly seemed to grow, making it a major obstacle to his continued bending. But the discomforts were as nothing to the pleasure of harvesting. Provided, he thought ruefully, that it didn't go on for too long . . .

When they reached the end of the row, he held the half-filled sack open and she tipped the beans from the two buckets into it. Then, despite her protests, he carried the sack to the casita where he put it down near the table; Monserrat watched him with sneering dislike.

'You'll have a drink?' she asked.

'That's a great idea.'

'Adolfo, would you . . .' She stopped, realizing the futility of asking her son to do anything. She went into the casita.

Alvarez thankfully sat. He looked out at the field and thought with grateful pride that just for a short time he had been allowed to remind himself of what life was really about.

When she returned, she carried a battered tin tray on which were three glasses of red wine. She offered the tray to Alvarez, who took a glass, then to her son.

'I don't want that muck.'

'But you know that's all there is.'

'Then I'll go and get something that's drinkable.' Monserrat stood, stamped off.

She said, very uneasy: 'It's true it's only homemade wine, señor. Perhaps you would rather not have it?'

'I would prefer it to anything else you could offer.'

She was both relieved and gratified.

He drank. The wine was raw and a connoisseur would no doubt have suddenly remembered a very pressing engagement, but he savoured every mouthful. It returned him to the days when he'd been sent along to the bodega with a jar that was filled with wine at a few centavos a litre.

After a while he said: 'Señora, while you've been working at Casa Gran in the past few weeks, have there been many visitors apart from the women?'

'Not really.'

'If I mentioned thugs, would you be able to picture what sort of person I was talking about?'

'I . . . Well, I think so.'

'It's the kind of man you take one look at and reckon you'd best not start an argument with. He doesn't have to be all muscle, just vicious.'

She nodded her head to show that now she fully understood.

'Have you seen someone like that at Casa Gran recently?'

'Never,' she answered immediately.

Her evidence hadn't taken things very far, but then he hadn't expected it to. If Roig had hired a contract man who had turned on him, it was reasonable to suppose that he'd have made as certain as possible that no one else saw them together. But if Oakley had been guilty of the murder and was intending to put forward the defence that Roig had been killed by a man he'd hired to kill, then her evidence might add just a little weight towards the demolition of such a defence.

She said deferentially: 'Your glass is empty, señor. I poured one out for Adolfo, but he didn't want it. Would you like it?'

He thanked her and picked up the full glass.

The outside door to Roig's office was slightly ajar and Alvarez pushed it open. Clearly, Marta, chewing gum, seated behind the reception desk, had imagined the door firmly closed and herself safe from observation, because she had propped up a copy of *¡Hola!* against the typewriter and was intently reading it. Then the door squeaked. Startled, she looked up, grabbed the magazine and dropped it on to her lap. 'What d'you want?' she demanded with guilty bad temper. Then she recognized him. 'Oh, it's you!' She smoothed out a page of the magazine which had become bent over and set it down by the side of the typewriter.

'There's something more I want to ask you.'

'Such as what?'

He moved a chair and sat.

'Make yourself at home.'

As he grew older, he understood the young less and less. He'd always shown respect to his elders, even when they'd been utter boors. But the young today didn't seem to know the meaning of the word respect—or of work, for that matter.

'You might tell me what you're on about—I haven't all day.'

'You are, perhaps, in a hurry to return to *¡Hola!*?'

She was, just for the moment, disconcerted.

'Señorita, did Señor Roig do much criminal work?'

'Some, but most of his work was for the foreigners because it was so much more profitable.' She spoke with knowing slyness.

'If I talk about a hard criminal, you'd understand the kind of person I mean?'

''Course I would.'

'Has there been such a man in this office in the past month?'

She shook her head.

'Has such a man consulted Señor Roig in the past year?'

'That's a different matter—I mean, you are talking about a long time.'

'You're saying that off-hand you can't be certain one way or the other?'

'You can't expect me to remember all that way back.'

'True. So that is why I'm going to ask you to go through all the records pertaining to the past year and to pick out the names of anyone who you think fits the description of a hard case.'

'That's an awful lot of hard work,' she complained bitterly.

On returning to his office, Alvarez found a message on the desk. The cabin personnel manager of Iberia had rung to say that the cabin staff would be at the airport at eleven the next morning and he was to be there sharp on time.

CHAPTER 17

The personnel manager turned out to be exactly the kind of woman Alvarez had visualized; sharp, lean looks which included a beaky nose, thin lips, and a body whose curves suggested cutting edges rather than rounded smoothness. 'It's taken a great deal of trouble to organize,' she snapped.

'I am sorry to have caused so much upset,' Alvarez answered.

'We've more than enough work to do as it is.'

'I can assure you that the matter is very important.'

'But it is not in the interests of flying . . . Come with me, please.'

She reminded him of the schoolmistress—in those days, one of the few on the island—who'd taught him mathematics; every mistake in reciting one's tables had resulted in a sharp slap from a heavy brass-edged ruler.

They entered a room, obviously heavily used, along one wall of which ran a coffee and snack bar, and along the opposite one a line of TV monitors. Four women and one man, all in Iberia uniform, were grouped around the bar.

'This is the inspector,' the personnel manager announced in tones of dissociation. She turned to Alvarez. 'You have fifteen minutes and no longer.'

'Thank you very much, señora, for all your help.'

She nodded, left.

'Left, right, left, right, straighten your backs,' said the smallest of the stewardesses.

'She's not so bad,' said the steward pacifically, his accent marking him to be a Madrileño.

'Not so bad as who—Dracula's aunt?'

The steward turned to Alvarez. 'Would you like a coffee, Inspector? I'm afraid there's nothing stronger served here.'

'A coffee would be very nice, but is there time?'

'Forget what she said; we've half an hour before we need to move.' He called out: 'José.' A man wearing a white apron came through the doorway behind the bar. 'Make it one more coffee, will you?' He turned to Alvarez. 'How would you like it?'

'Cortado, please.'

'What say we sit?'

Once they were seated, the younger of the two blonde stewardesses said: 'What's all this about, Inspector?'

'I'm going to ask all of you, señorita, if you can identify a man as having flown to Heathrow a week ago last Tuesday.

'That's really asking!'

'He was first class.'

'Even so, you're talking about nearly a fortnight ago.'

'Come on, Cati,' said the brunette on her right, 'this ought to be right up your street. You're always telling us what a wonderful memory you've got.'

'Wonderful, but not computer-infallible.'

José came round the bar and up to the table, placed a cup and saucer in front of Alvarez, who reached down to his trouser pocket. The steward said: 'Forget it . . . Put it down on my slate.'

José left.

The second blonde—the roots of her hair more noticeably darker than those of her companion—said to Alvarez: 'What's the case you're interested in?'

'The murder of a man called Roig.'

The steward whistled. 'I read about that in the local

paper. There was a photograph of the house and it looked
like a mansion.'

'Is the man you're interested in the murderer?' asked the
elder blonde.

Alvarez shook his head. 'Nothing as definite as that. In
fact, at this stage, we don't even know for sure that he's
connected with the case, but as I guess you'll know, we have
to follow up all sorts of leads.' He produced a photograph
—it was an enlarged reproduction of the one in Oakley's
passport—and handed it to the steward.

The steward passed on the photograph. 'Have I got this
right? You want to know if this man was on Flight 628 a
week ago last Tuesday?'

'That's it.'

'As Cati said a moment ago, it's some question! We do
more than one short-haul flight a day and so one becomes
very much like another . . .'

The second blonde interrupted him. 'Except when one of
the passengers is threatening to have a baby.'

They laughed; clearly, they'd recently experienced such
a situation.

'What I'm hoping,' said Alvarez, 'is that on the Tuesday
something—probably not so dramatic as that!—did happen
which will enable you to fix the flight in your minds. One
thing is, although the first class was completely booked, one
passenger didn't show.'

'Completely booked?' said the steward. 'That's unusual
even at this time of the year, when economy is bulging at
the seams . . .' He tailed off into silence.

'Isn't that the day the champagne ran out because there
were so many in first and the old bitch with a fortune in
diamonds on her fingers became so rude?' suggested one of
the brunettes.

'I reckon it must be,' said the steward, after a while.
'Everyone seemed to be on champagne and I hadn't checked
stocks. And that old battleaxe threatened to report us all to

the director, the prime minister, and anyone else she could think of. And when I put in a report on the incident—just in case she did create a stink—José María remarked that that sort of thing always seems to happen on a Tuesday . . . Right, I think we've nailed down the flight. Was this bloke aboard?' The photograph had been returned to him and he picked it up and looked at it for several seconds. 'I certainly don't recall seeing him.'

None of them remembered Oakley; Cati, perhaps determined to bolster her claim of a very good memory, stated categorically that he had not flown with them.

Indicative, thought Alvarez, but very far from conclusive.

London rang at ten-fifteen on Saturday morning.

'Mallinson here,' said the cheerful inspector. 'It's still raining and we're all beginning to grow webbed feet . . . We've done what we can for you, but I don't think you'll find as much cheer in what I've got to tell you as you probably hoped. When the passport was issued eight years ago, Oakley was living in Bromley. We visited the address and spoke to people who might be able to help. I don't know if you've any idea of what life's often like for a lot of people in a place like that? Half the time it's superficial, the other half it's empty; people come and people go and precious few roots are put down; friendships are only as deep as seems worthwhile and neighbours are barely on nodding terms across the garden fence. So after one year there's no one can remember much, and after two or three . . . The Oakleys weren't gregarious and didn't join in the social rounds. He's described as pleasant and good-humoured, but rather reserved, she as more extrovert; according to one person, she was on the stage before she married. Incidentally, there was no suggestion of any rift between them; quite the contrary, in fact—in the days of energetic wife-swapping, they were noted spoilsports. There's one daughter, attractive, bright, who trained at RADA—that's a drama school;

following in her mother's footsteps, perhaps. Their lifestyle was comfortable, but not ostentatiously wealthy.

'The people who bought the house from them still own it. They've had no contact with them since the sale was completed and they can't remember any mention of where the Oakleys were moving to beyond a vague impression that they were going abroad.

'The estate agents have had no further contact with them, the post office were paid for six weeks to redirect any mail to the local Lloyds Bank and the bank has no record now of where they sent the redirected mail. Some four months after the house was sold, the two accounts with Lloyds were closed down and the money transferred to a Swiss bank.'

Alvarez said, a little hesitantly: 'Could all this suggest they deliberately set out to hide their tracks?'

'It's impossible to say. They've certainly drawn a curtain behind them, but a lot of people do that without ever setting out to do so and there's nothing here to say whether it's happened deliberately or fortuitously.'

'Then you were right and there isn't any help. But thank you for all your trouble.'

'Hang on. As a matter of fact, what I actually said was, as much cheer as you'd probably hoped. But in another respect we have learned something worthwhile. Oakley worked in the City for a firm of stockbrokers. That firm was swallowed up by another, but quite a few of the staff stayed on with the new concern and one of them was able to tell us that Oakley quite definitely had personal dealings with the man who's the suspect in the insider dealing case. So there's little doubt that Oakley uses information from London to make money, then launders this money through Ashley Developments.'

'Are you any nearer being able to prove that?'

'Not at the moment. I don't have to tell you that surmises on their own never put a guilty man behind bars—and hell, at this stage we can't even go so far as to prove there's

been insider trading, thanks to the blasted laws of Cayman
Islands.'

'Is there no chance of persuading someone over there to
leak the information you need?'

'Perish the idea! Imagine the screams from the pink
loonies in Parliament if the news ever got out. No, at the
moment we can see only two ways of moving forward.
Either, when our chap comes over to you and questions
Oakley, he manages to learn something incriminating, or
you can corner Oakley and persuade him that it's in his
interests to talk. Perhaps the promise of a slightly lighter
sentence—if that's possible.'

'Is that an official request?'

Mallinson laughed. 'Nothing so definite. Merely a vague
thought.'

'Talking about your chap coming over, is there any date
fixed yet?'

'Only as soon as possible—and I know that that doesn't
answer your question. But I gather there's so much work in
hand it's proving very difficult to find anyone who can be
spared for a few days; fraud's booming, if nothing else is.'

A couple of minutes later, the call was over and Alvarez
relaxed in the chair. Yet again, evidence was inconclusive.
Oakley might have deliberately set out to disappear from
sight, on the other hand there could be no certainty. But,
remembering that it was now all but certain that Oakley,
through Ashley Developments, was working hand-in-glove
with the man engaged in insider dealing, it surely was more
likely that the result had been intended.

He yawned, looked at his watch. Almost two and a half
hours before he could break off for lunch . . .

Alvarez drove into Palma on Monday morning, parked in
the underground car park at Plaza Major, and from there
walked to Roig's office. On this occasion, Marta was busy
typing.

'You look as if you're back in business,' he said.

'The señora's arranged for someone else to take over the business and I'm to get everything up to date.'

'And is that a bit of a job?'

She had been prepared to be as bad-tempered and unco-operative as before, but his friendliness disarmed her. 'It's more than that . . . And the señora's no idea how much more. To listen to her talking, I'll finish by this evening.'

He sat on the edge of the desk. She told him that even though it seemed the new man might offer to keep her on, she didn't know that she'd accept. Working for a solicitor was hard and often boring and sometimes she became so depressed because of all the troubles that she had to deal with that she didn't think she could carry on.

He sympathized with her, then said: 'Have you had a chance to look out those names for me?'

'Yeah. It took ages.'

'I was afraid it might. I'm really grateful. How many cases have you found?'

'Five.' She hesitated. 'You did talk about really vicious men—it wasn't just someone picking a pocket or mugging a tourist?'

'That's exactly right. The kind of brutal crime which makes you draw in your breath when you hear about it.'

'Then it is only the five. Like I told you, the señor preferred to work for the foreigners.' She searched the top of her desk, then opened the top right-hand drawer and brought out a folder from which she extracted a sheet of paper. 'There are the names.'

He took the paper from her. 'Again, many thanks.'

She smiled and suddenly no longer looked fretful and slightly bad-tempered.

He left the office and returned to the traffic-clogged street. Five names, none of which he recognized. Immediately, he decided, he'd hold them in reserve. But the moment it began to look as if the motive for Roig's murder was none of the more obvious ones, then he'd ask Records for full details on the five men and would check them out . . .

He drove out of the car park and along the Ronda to the Manacor road.

The receptionist at Hotel Rocador told Alvarez that Vidal was on bar duty at the pool. He walked through the lobby and the large lounge, out to the patio. Being on top of a cliff, at the base of which was virtually no beach, a swimming pool was a very important amenity—the hotel had two, one very large and one much smaller and constantly shallow for children. The large pool was clover-leaf-shaped and on the side of one of the 'leaves' a bar had been built out into the water; around this were fixed underwater bar stools. Vidal, and another employee, were serving in the bar.

Alvarez went up to the edge of the pit in which the bar stood, and called to Vidal, who looked at him, nodded disdainfully, and continued to mix a drink for a topless red head. Alvarez walked over to a chair set in the shade of an acacia. He stared at the sunbathers, each stretched out on chaise-longue, lilo, or towel, and wondered what his mother would have said had she been told that one day young women would come to the island who would be so brazen that they'd strip off almost naked in public? Perhaps it would be more to the point to wonder what his father would have said! . . .

Some ten minutes later, Vidal climbed out of the bar on to the poolside grama grass, which felt like cardboard underfoot. A young woman, lying on her back on a towel and displaying shapely breasts, raised herself on her elbows and spoke to him. Even at a distance, it was clear that she was asking him to do something and he was treating her request with indifference. These days the young, thought Alvarez, with sudden middle-aged jealous bad temper, had everything in life far too easily; when he'd been young, he'd have danced barefoot on glass to be spoken to by so attractive and unclad a woman.

Vidal was wearing an open-necked white shirt and sharply creased black trousers; he looked smart, handsome, and very self-possessed. 'You'd like a word with me?' he asked, his polite tone in sharp contrast to his expression.

'That's right.'

'Unfortunately, señor, as you saw, I am on duty.'

'I've had a word with management and it's OK for you to break off.'

'You told them why you wanted to speak to me?'

'I merely said I'd some routine questions; it sounded more tactful. You'd better find yourself a chair; we may be some time.'

'Of course. Excuse me for a moment.'

If only he weren't so damned polite, in a condescending manner!

Vidal brought over a chair, set it down, sat. 'I am ready,' he said, as if nothing of importance could begin until he was.

'Have you seen Señorita Garcia in the past couple of days?'

'I have not.'

'Why not? She's lonely, she's had a very rough time, and you're a cousin.'

'I am her second cousin.'

'And in Andalucia does that make all the difference? As a second cousin, you can forget her and leave her to her misery? You don't feel as we do, that a blood relationship, however remote, creates ties that should be honoured?' Their previous meeting had convinced Alvarez that the only way of breaking through Vidal's proud self-possession was to make him too angry to realize what he was saying.

Vidal's manner became sharply antagonistic. 'What would you know about how I feel?'

'Only by judging from your behaviour.'

'If . . .' He stopped.

'Well?'

'Nothing.'

'Were you going to say that if only she hadn't had an affair with Roig, you'd have rushed to comfort her? So is your pride the kind that's very fierce but fragile? Let anyone so much as criticize your second cousin with an unsullied reputation for the way she does her hair and you'll explode with prideful wrath; but if she's had the bad luck to end up in a situation that you think lowers her in the eyes of others, you walk away, however desperately she needs help, in case her misfortune begins to rub off on to you.'

'If you weren't a bloody policeman . . .'

'What would you do? Run your sword through my guts?'

Vidal stared at him for several seconds, then shrugged his shoulders.

Blast! thought Alvarez. Under provocation, Vidal had lost his hair-trigger temper—but he had then almost as quickly regained it. There was a sharpness there which was not always apparent . . . 'How many times have you been to Casa Gran?'

'Twice.'

'When?'

'I've told you before.'

'Why did you go to see Roig?'

'On a personal matter.'

'Was it to talk about Señorita Garcia?'

'I've just said, it was a personal matter.'

'There's something I can't begin to understand.'

After a while, Vidal said hoarsely: 'What?'

'Why you hadn't warned her about him?'

'D'you think I didn't try when I first heard? I told her exactly what kind of a man he was: a mujeriego.'

'What's that mean?'

'It's an Andaluce expression for a man who has seduced a gipsy woman and refuses to marry her and so make the liaison honourable in the eyes of the family; only his castration can restore the family's honour.'

Alvarez was startled. 'Castration restores honour! . . . So you were really telling her what you were going to do to Roig?'

'No.'

'Why not?'

'None of the families in Bodón or Posuna could know what had happened.'

'But you knew.'

'Would I tell anyone and bring shame to our family?'

Clearly, honour was impugned not by an act of dishonour, but by the publication of that act. 'On your second visit, did you call Roig a mujeriego to his face?'

'Maybe. I don't remember.'

'You don't? Perhaps one doesn't remember much about one's inferiors. Did you speak to the woman?'

'After the whore laughed at me, I told her she was a mala zorra.'

'Another Andaluce expression?'

'A diseased prostitute wouldn't soil her hands by touching a mala zorra.'

'You explained the meaning of the words to them?'

'Yes.'

'Then one can imagine he was somewhat angry. Did he threaten you?'

'Why do you keep asking the same questions?'

'Have I asked that one before? Then let's see if you give the same answer. Did he threaten you?'

'I didn't bother to listen to his ranting. I left.'

'Determined to teach him a lesson at a later date?'

'One doesn't bother to teach a cur.'

'Did you see Señorita Garcia after that?'

'No.'

'But she tried to get in touch with you, didn't she?'

'Perhaps.'

'She begged you to help her?'

'I had warned her.'

'In your proud world, is there no room for human weakness and emotional fallibility?'

'In my world, a woman does not dishonour herself with a mujeriego.'

'You've obviously yet to learn that sooner or later life kicks everyone in the crutch; even the proudest. And when one's really hurt, the sympathy of someone, someone even as low as a mala zorra, is infinitely more valuable than the justification of a proud and honourable man . . . But I don't suppose you've the slightest interest in what I'm trying to tell you. Each generation refuses to learn except by harsh experience. That's the real tragedy of life.'

'You sound like a preacher.'

'There can be worse comparisons . . . Where were you on the night of the murder?'

'I told you.'

'Tell me again.'

'In my room because I was off duty.'

'Nowhere else?'

'I said I might have gone to a bar; I can't remember.'

'Did your landlady see you at all?'

'No.'

'Can anyone vouch for you . . . And don't bother to remind me that an Andaluce gentleman does not lie.'

'I can't remember anyone.'

'It would pay you to.'

He shrugged his shoulders.

Alvarez stood. 'Suppose you stop thinking about your sense of honour and try to imagine how much some real sympathy would mean to the señorita?'

Vidal's expression became stubborn.

CHAPTER 18

On Tuesday morning, when Alvarez arrived at La Portaña, climbed out of his car, and stared around the urbanización, it was clear that the tempo of work had slowed. The cranes looming over the blocks of flats were not operating, the grass in the square, previously so neatly trimmed, was now in need of cutting, none of the sprinklers was operating, and no gardeners were working on the flowerbeds.

He entered the office. The over-groomed young man was not there and it was the typist who came up to the counter. He asked if Vich was free.

Vich called him into the inner office. Vich's manner was subdued and therefore he was not surprised when, once they were seated, the other said: 'Since you were last here, things haven't improved.'

'I gathered there'd been a bit of a slowdown.'

'I left a solid job to come and work for this outfit; trouble was, it didn't pay all that well. Like a bloody fool, I remembered all the moans of the wife and kids because we couldn't afford this and that, things that other people had, and I decided to make the change . . . Now, every time I look in a mirror I see someone who's soon going to be out of work.'

'It's rough,' said Alvarez sympathetically.

'I'm not saying any of us is going to starve. The wife's family have a couple of fincas and we could go and live in one of 'em and farm. I come from farming stock and don't mind getting my hands mucky. But the kids would hate like hell to have to leave Palma and live out in the sticks and the wife would miss all her friends; and it's a fact that I wouldn't fancy being beholden to her family. Nice enough people if you don't owe them anything, but if you do, do they let you know about it!'

'Isn't there still time for the money to be found?'

'Not enough. Not with the banks and the other property company so keen to take over.'

'No joy from Ashley Developments?'

'If they were going to do anything, surely they'd have done it before now?'

One man committed a swindle, thought Alvarez, and an ever-growing number of people were affected, many of them people the swindler didn't even know existed; crime was as cruel indirectly as directly.

'But you didn't come to listen to me moaning,' said Vich, trying to be more cheerful. 'So how can I help you?'

'Last time I was here, I mentioned a man called Gerald Oakley, but you said then that you'd never come across him. Have you done so since?'

'No. Would you have expected me to?'

'I don't really know,' replied Alvarez slowly. Oakley might want to save Andreu y Soler, but all his energies were surely far more likely to be engaged in trying to save himself from a charge of murder.

Mallinson rang from London at six-fifteen. 'Sergeant Farley has been released from the case he was on and will be coming out to question Oakley—that's with your permission, of course. He'll be arriving tomorrow evening on CT 3164, a charter flight, arriving at Palma at seven-fifteen. Is there any chance you can arrange for him to be met?'

'I will be there myself.'

'That's great. And as it's probably going to take a little time, he'll need a hotel for a few days; will you book him in somewhere?'

'It may be a little difficult at this time of the season to find him a nice room, but I'll do my best.'

'There's no need for anything too nice; after all, he's only a sergeant.' Mallinson laughed.

*

Farley was large and jovial and Alvarez, who met him in the arrival hall, liked him on sight. They chatted as they waited for the luggage to arrive on the carousel—as always, this took a considerable time because many of the handlers were having coffee—and then left, waved through the Customs check-point by a guard who knew Alvarez.

Once settled in his car, Alvarez looked at his watch. 'It's just after eight, so we can either have supper here in Palma, or drive back to Llueso which will take an hour, and eat there. Which would you prefer?'

'As a matter of fact, I am a bit peckish because we were only given biscuits and what they said was coffee on the plane, but I leave it to you.'

'Then we will stay here and eat at Celler Tomás. Their lomo con col is superb.'

'Fine, just so long as what you've mentioned doesn't contain snails.'

'You don't like them? But cooked the Mallorquin way, they're delicious.'

'Despite having a French grandmother, I just cannot face the thought of having one of them wink at me just before I go to bite it.'

It was a pity, Alvarez thought, that the English had never learned to take their food seriously.

Celler Tomás was in the centre of Palma and although discerning foreigners—that is, those who did not require table linen and obsequious waiters—often ate there, it was not a tourist restaurant. Farley pronounced the lomo con col delicious; he also said that the second carafe of red wine was even better than the first. And by the time he was enjoying a brandy with the coffee, he was becoming very interested in the cost of houses on the island. Ten minutes after they left the underground car park, and before they reached the autoroute, he was asleep and he did not awaken until they were beyond Inca and the eastern sky was almost dark.

'Ye gods!' he said, as he sat upright.

'Is something wrong?'

'I've been asleep. I'm terribly sorry. I meant to talk over the case with you.'

'Tomorrow's soon enough,' said Alvarez, surprised.

Farley might not have heard him. 'It's the heat and all that wine with the meal; I'm just not used to it.'

What was life when there was no sun and no wine?

The hotel was on the eastern end of the front in Puerto Llueso; from most of the bedrooms one looked across the bay to the mountains which ringed the far side, a view that was always changing its colours, always beautiful.

On the following morning Alvarez took the lift to the fifth and top floor and walked along the corridor to the end room. He knocked, entered. Farley, stripped to the waist, was sunbathing out on the small balcony. 'I'm damned if I knew there was anywhere on the island half as lovely as this. I'd heard it was all concrete.'

Alvarez spoke sadly. 'If some people have their way, it will be, even here in Puerto Llueso.' The pace of development in the port was accelerating after years during which it had been carefully held in check. No one seemed to know quite why the change. There was talk of bribes given and fortunes made, but talk came easily. Certainly, the building provided work for many people, but if all the quiet charm was destroyed and in consequence the number of visitors dropped—those who sought brash entertainment would always look for it elsewhere—then long-term it could turn out to be a very expensive solution to the problem of unemployment. 'Shall we go and speak to Oakley?'

'I'll be with you just as soon as I've put on a shirt.'

'By the way, I would be careful; it is very easy to become badly sunburned.'

Farley stepped from the balcony into the bedroom, crossed to the nearer bed, and picked up his shirt. 'Thanks

for the warning, but in fact I don't suppose I'll get the
chance to overdo things. I've a mountain of work waiting
on my desk, so I have to get back just as soon as I possibly
can.' He noticed the expression on Alvarez's face and
chuckled. 'You think that's crazy?'

'A very commendable attitude, but . . .'

'But why kill myself rushing?' He turned and looked
through the window. 'Another twenty-four hours of this sort
of life and I reckon I won't know the answer. Who the hell
really cares if half the City is defrauding the other half, just
so long as I can lie out in the sun, swim in a warm sea, and
have a couple of bottles of wine with every meal!'

They drove to Ca'n Tardich.

Farley studied the house. 'If this is where insider trading
gets you, lead me inside.'

They crossed to the front door and Alvarez knocked.
Beatriz opened it. He greeted her, then said with mild
curiosity: 'What are you doing here today? I thought your
days were Mondays, Wednesdays, and Fridays?'

'The señor wanted me to give the house a really good
clean through and asked if I could put in a bit of extra time.'

'Is he in?'

She shook her head.

'Have you any idea when he'll be back?'

'Only that it probably won't be before lunch.'

Alvarez spoke to Farley in English, explaining what had
happened, then turned back to Beatriz. 'I suppose you've
no idea where he's gone?'

'I haven't, no.'

'Then we'll return this evening and see if he's back . . .
Will you leave a message and say we'll be around at about
six? And if he can't make it then, would he please be certain
to be here tomorrow morning at nine-thirty.'

They returned to the car. 'Strewth, but it's hot!' said
Farley, as he settled in the car and clipped up the safety-belt.
'I feel as if I'm dissolving.'

'Since now there is nothing you can do until this evening, why not cool down in the sea?'

'Why not indeed!'

They returned to Ca'n Tardich at six-ten that evening. The air was filled with the shrilling of cicadas, the croaking call of frogs, intermittently sounding sheep bells, and the barking of dogs tied up at the entrance of fields to 'guard' them. Up in the sharp blue sky, two aircraft created crossing white plumes as they overflew the island in different directions.

Alvarez knocked on the front door. There was no reply.

'Not back yet,' said Farley.

'Or he's gone out again.'

'Would he, if he'd got your message?'

'Beatriz may not have left it; she likes him and thinks I shouldn't keep bothering him. We islanders don't take much notice of authority.' Alvarez spoke with both pride and irritation. He walked over to the garage and looked through the crack between the two doors. 'The car's away.' He scratched his chin. 'Just to make sure tomorrow, I'll ring first thing in the morning and say he's not to leave here until we've spoken to him.'

'I don't see how he'll be able to wriggle out of that.'

'So now we have to make two decisions. Which bar do we go to for a drink, and to which restaurant for a meal?'

'Tell me something, Enrique: living here, how in the hell do you ever get any work done?'

'It is a question I occasionally ask myself.'

Alvarez crumbled a slice of coca into the hot chocolate which was well laced with brandy. Dolores dried one of the plates she had just washed. 'It's María's First Communion next week.'

'Which María's that?'

'Typical!' she told the plate. 'Only a man could ask, which María!'

'But we know so many.'

'Cecilia's María, that's which. Such a sweet little thing.'

It was not the description he would have given the young girl whose manners so often proved that she'd been spoiled from the day she'd been born.

'I've said I'll help with the cooking for the party which means being out all day, so you'll have to get your own lunch.'

He showed his astonishment.

'It won't kill you for once.'

Maybe it wouldn't, but what counted was the principle. In the old days, no woman would for one second have considered leaving her menfolk to provide their own lunch. He'd always been against joining the Common Market.

'Cecilia told me that they're getting the baker to cook four suckling pigs.'

'Four?'

'They want to have a good party.'

'But however many people are they asking?'

'Hundreds,' she answered, careless of the real number.

He ate another spoonful of coca and chocolate. Parties on christenings, First Communions, weddings, and Saints' Days, were becoming bigger and bigger as each giver vied to present the most Lucullan feast. A far cry from his First Communion: just a few pasties filled with angels'-hair jam and homemade wine . . .

She said: 'Will you get your present separately or would you rather join in with us?'

'It'll be a lot easier if I join in with you.'

'Then you'd better give me five thousand pesetas.'

'How much?'

'You don't want us to appear mean, do you?' She stared hard at him, then resumed washing up. 'I've decided to buy her a frock; there are two I really like in that new shop next to the bank.'

'It's a very expensive place.'

'The blue one is lovely, but it does cost a bit more than I'd reckoned on. I suppose the green one is almost as nice and it is a lot cheaper, but . . .'

'I think she's always looked most attractive in green.'

She said with good-tempered scorn: 'As if you've ever noticed what colour she's been wearing!' She turned. 'You're bringing the Englishman to lunch, aren't you?'

'If that's still all right with you?'

'I don't suppose he'll like my cooking.'

'On the contrary. I told him, you're the finest cook on the island.'

She accepted that compliment without any sense of modesty.

'I said that your hunters' quail have flown straight down from heaven.'

This further compliment provoked a rare touch of self-criticism. 'The last time there was something not quite right. Perhaps not quite enough sobrasada . . .'

He looked up at the electric clock on the wall and realized that time was getting on and if he was to be certain of speaking to Oakley, he'd better phone now. He left the kitchen and went through to the front room and the telephone. The call went unanswered. The agreement had been to pick up Farley on the way to Ca'n Tardich, but he decided to go straight there.

The front door of the house was locked and the garage was empty. If Beatriz had left the message, Oakley's absence was deliberate and he was probably on the run; but if through carelessness, or pig-headedness, she had not passed on the message, then his absence was probably without any special significance . . .

He drove back to Llueso and parked outside No. 21, Calle General Riera. Beatriz, obviously about to leave for work and impatient to be on her way, said: 'Of course I gave him your message.'

'He returned before you left?'

'He did not. I put the message where I always do when there's something to tell him, but he's out.'

'What exactly did you write?'

She said, becoming uneasy instead of belligerent: 'Just that you'd called with an Englishman and wanted him to be in the house either that evening or this morning.'

The reference to an Englishman would have alerted Oakley, but he had no passport . . .

'Is there anything more you want?' she asked.

He shook his head.

'Then is it all right if I'm on my way?'

A moment later she wheeled a Mobylette out of the house, started it, and drove off. He watched her round the corner and go out of sight. The first thing to do was to telephone Emigration and warn them that a passportless Oakley might try to slip past (assuming he hadn't already done so) and . . . Suddenly it occurred to him that on the plea of a lost passport, Oakley might have applied to the British Consulate for temporary papers; they had not been warned not to issue any . . .

He hurried back to his office and telephoned the consulate. In the past week only two people had applied for temporary papers, following the theft of their passports, and neither was Oakley. Imagining what Salas could have found to say if Oakley had successfully chosen that means of escape, Alvarez breathed a deep sigh of relief. He spoke to Emigration. There was no way Oakley could have left.

He returned downstairs and as he drew level with the duty desk, the cabo seated behind it said: 'There was a message for you earlier on. The harbour master reports that one of the yachts has been taken.'

CHAPTER 19

By the time Alvarez reached the hotel, Farley was out on the patio which jutted out over the sandy beach, drinking a mid-morning coffee.

'I'm sorry to be so late,' Alvarez said, 'but things have started moving very fast.' He sat at the table. 'I telephoned Oakley's house earlier on, but there wasn't any reply so I went straight there, instead of coming here first. The house was locked and the car was out. Then I had a word with Beatriz and she assured me she'd left the message and he must have seen it. In it, she mentioned I'd been with an Englishman. That obviously alerted him. I was just leaving the station to come here when I received a message to the effect that a yacht'd disappeared from the harbour.'

'Does anyone know at what time it went?'

'At the moment, I've told you all I know.'

'Then you'll be in a hurry to start asking questions.' Farley lifted his cup and drained it. 'Lead on.'

They drove round to the eastern arm of the harbour and parked half way along this. 'The harbour master's office is just beyond the restaurant,' said Alvarez, 'but first it'll be an idea to check the cars.'

Cars were parked wherever there was space. The white Seat 127 was the last one before the tables and chairs set outside the yacht club. The driving door was unlocked. On the front passenger seat was a plastic shopping-bag with the logo of Continente, from which had spilled a quarter kilo pack of butter; in the heat—the sun was beating through the side windows—the butter had begun to melt and a small yellow rivulet had spread across the cloth.

'Been shopping,' said Farley, 'returned home, went indoors without unloading everything, read the note, and promptly took off.'

'So now we must speak with the harbour master.'

The harbour master was not in the small air-conditioned office, but his young and engagingly helpful assistant was and he gave them what information he could. 'Roughly an hour ago, Señor Cassell came in and wanted to know where his yacht was; very pugnacious about it.'

'And then?'

'I went with him to his berth, but that was certainly empty. So I had a quick look round the harbour to make certain some bloody fool joker hadn't merely shifted her.'

'Was it fit to go to sea?'

'The señor's a real yachtsman, unlike some of the owners of the floating gin palaces who hardly know which end of the boat is which; his yacht is always ready to sail.'

'Would it be big enough to reach the mainland?'

The assistant spoke with cheerful contempt for such ignorance. 'It's never merely a question of size, it's how the yacht's built and who's sailing her. A couple of good seamen could sail the señor's yacht right round the world.'

'Then could one man handle it?'

'She; a boat's always feminine because you don't know how she's going to behave next . . . Yeah, someone who knows what he's doing could easily sail her. All I was really saying was, on a long passage it's safer and easier with two.'

Alvarez told Farley in English what had been said.

'Where d'you reckon he'll be making for?' asked Farley.

'Almost certainly not Menorca, Ibiza, or Formentera, since he must know they'll be alerted. But as to how much further afield . . .?'

'How far is it to France?'

Alvarez put the question to the assistant, who went over to the chart table, opened a drawer and brought out a chart, then used dividers to measure the distance, which he set against the latitude scale. 'Call it a hundred and eighty nautical miles from here to Port Vendres.'

'What sort of speed would the yacht be making?'

'In a light wind like this?' He looked out through the window at the bay. 'With plenty of sail hoisted, four knots at the very most. But that's guesswork. You'll have to speak to the señor to find out more precisely how she makes in these conditions.'

'Does she have a motor?'

'Bound to have, but that'll be only for docking, emergencies, or charging the batteries. She'll make better way under sail.'

Again, Alvarez translated.

'What's the earliest time at which she could have been stolen?' Farley asked.

The assistant said that the señor had been aboard, splicing some ropes, until around eight, when he'd returned home. She could have been taken any time after that.

Farley looked at his watch. 'That gives a maximum of fifteen hours; give her three to four knots and she's forty-five to sixty miles away—in other words, she can't have reached the mainland.'

'Before a search can be ordered,' said Alvarez, 'I have to inform my superior chief of what has happened and before I do that I need at least two brandies. So we need to add on a couple of miles, at least.'

Salas was surprisingly calm. He said that in the circumstances Alvarez had done almost as much as a competent officer would have done and agreed it would have been impossible to keep a constant watch on all the yachts in Llueso harbour, even more impossible on those in all the other harbours as well. There was a puzzled look on Alvarez's face as he replaced the receiver.

The decision had to be made where to search, accepting that the resources available were very limited. The Peninsula offered the nearest coast, but the police there could act immediately and there would be none of the delays—potentially so valuable to Oakley—which could occur once national boundaries were crossed. France was reasonably near, but was the most obvious country. Of those further away and politically possible, Italy, Greece, and Turkey, lay to the east and each, for different reasons, could prove an attractive haven; Morocco, Algeria, Tunisia and Egypt were to the south and east, and while it might not be so easy to lose oneself in one of them, extradition would be more difficult or impossible. Gibraltar, Portugal, and the Americas, lay to the west . . . Alvarez decided on France, his reasoning being simple. When Oakley stole the yacht (not knowing the owner lived locally), he must have hoped that its disappearance would go unnoticed for a long time —obviously, the empty berth would be remarked, but unless by the owner or friends of his (many boats were owned by people who lived abroad and only came out for holidays) then this would cause no comment. But, being a clever man, he accepted that Sod's Law was always waiting to strike and the disappearance might well be noticed much sooner than expected, so that the quicker he was ashore in another country, the better . . .

The harbour master and Cassell—belligerent, damning Alvarez for allowing his beloved craft to be stolen—conferred about winds, currents, distances through water as opposed to over the land, ability to sail into the wind, and amount of sail one man would prudently carry, and determined a figure that gave the radius of a circle, centred on Puerto Llueso. The course to Port Vendres was plotted and the point at which this cut the radius of the circle was named as the yacht's position in one hour's time.

A seaplane, normally used to 'bomb' forest fires with several tonnes of sea water, took off from Llueso Bay and headed eastwards, climbing steadily.

Sometimes, the needle in the haystack is found. At 14.12

hours, the crew sighted a yacht, heading north. They went down and circled her, radioed the number on her mainsail; it was confirmed that she was the yacht they had sought. They were ordered to remain on station until a fast naval patrol boat reached the scene.

They began the boring task of circling the yacht as she sailed steadily on. It was soon remarked that there was no sign of life aboard.

CHAPTER 20

'Well?' said Salas, over the phone.

Alvarez began to tap on the desk with his fingers. 'The cabin's been checked for prints and his have been found; Señor Cassell says that at no time has he ever been invited aboard. It must have been he who stole the yacht.'

'So?'

'Then on the face of things he must have fallen overboard and by now be presumed drowned. The safety harness had been rigged, but the harness itself was lying on deck. Señor Cassell says that in fine weather, with very little sea, there's always the temptation to work on deck without wearing a harness. But it's easy to slip and fall overboard and with the sails set and the self-steering engaged, and no one else aboard to bring it back, there's absolutely no hope. You just watch it sail out of sight as you wait to drown . . . A horrible thought, isn't it?'

Salas seldom concerned himself with horrible thoughts. 'What lifeboats or rafts were there?'

'One liferaft, kept in a metal container lashed on deck, and one small inflatable. Both were still aboard.'

'Could he have left the yacht soon after clearing the port, leaving it to sail on unmanned?'

'I've checked on that point. Until not long before the

yacht was sighted, the wind was more westerly. I don't understand all the reasoning, but Señor Cassell and the harbour master insist that the fact that the yacht was found where she was shows she was under command until a short time before she was sighted; say a couple of hours. That's borne out by the meal. There was always some tinned food aboard and some baked beans had been opened and heated; these were cold, but they had not begun to dry out on the surface.'

'Then the suggestion has to be that he'd started to eat, something happened up on deck which alerted him, he went up, and in dealing with the trouble he fell overboard because he hadn't bothered to don the safety harness?'

'Indeed, señor. And it is fact that a boat-hook was loose and rolling about because a lashing had frayed.'

'But you don't agree with so logical a conclusion?'

'I can't help thinking that it would be very convenient for him if he could persuade us that he was dead.'

'I thought you'd just assured me that he must have sailed the boat out of port and until something like two hours before it was sighted?'

'Yes, but might he not have set the scene to make us think that he'd fallen overboard whereas in reality he was picked up by a fast powerboat and whisked away? . . . Eventually, of course, the truth will probably be discoverable through studying the business dealings of Ashley Developments; although it's very doubtful that we shall ever gain permission . . .'

Salas shouted: 'I know exactly what you're trying to do. Didn't I warn you at the beginning of the case?'

'About what, señor?'

'About complicating every bloody thing in sight. You've buried and resurrected this Englishman so many times I've lost count and now, goddamn it, you want to do both at the same time.' He slammed down the receiver.

For a time it had seemed that Salas was becoming a

patient man, ready to listen to reason; the last few moments had proved this not to be so. Alvarez was relieved. Change so often presaged trouble.

An assistant from the forensic laboratory rang on Saturday morning. 'We've examined the passport. We lifted off the paper without any trouble, but the original entry had been carefully erased and bringing that up proved a bit more difficult. The name is Mrs Stephanie Oakley and the address is Flat 64, 58 Via Santa Lucia, San Remo, Italy. There's no telephone number.'

'You what?' demanded Salas, in tones of disbelief.

'I'd like to go to Italy, señor,' replied Alvarez.

'And so would I. Regrettably, I don't find it nearly so easy to ignore the demands of my work.'

'If the señora is still living there, she needs to be questioned.'

'That is obvious. What is far less obvious is why you don't propose to ask the Italian police to find out whether she's still at that address.'

'That wouldn't be nearly so satisfactory.'

'To you?'

'To finding out the facts. I might be able to tell if she's speaking the truth, but if the Italian police question her they cannot judge because they will not know all the background; and if they do question her first and in consequence of what they report, we then decide I must question her as well, she will be forewarned.'

'It doesn't occur to you that in view of what Oakley said about his marriage, it's extremely unlikely she will be able to help and therefore the questioning of her is purely a formality, capable of being carried out by anyone?'

'But if he is still alive, might he not have lied about the state of his marriage, as he has about so many other things?'

'Why the devil should he have done?'

'I don't know, señor.'

'And nor, goddamnit, does anyone else.'

CHAPTER 21

Varessi, who'd pompously introduced himself at the airport as an officer of the Criminal Investigation Department of the Carabinieri, did not, on the car journey, try to hide his belief that Mallorca was a very distant land; he asked whether television had yet reached the island and was surprised to discover that it had, years before. He was a reckless driver, even by Italian standards, and Alvarez, at times himself inclined to ignore other road users, frequently called silently but fervently on St Christopher.

They raced into San Remo, swooped down and up the undulating road, and then climbed towards the back of the town as if engaged on a mountain race. They cut across a van to enter Via Santa Lucia and drew up with a screech of tyres.

'A very beautiful building,' said Varessi, as he looked up through the window. 'I doubt you have anything like this in Mallorca.'

The tall, ugly block of flats would not have been out of place in El Arenal, but Alvarez made no comment. In the first place, correcting Varessi was a long and difficult task; secondly, although he could understand Italian reasonably well, he found it difficult to speak; Varessi spoke neither English nor French.

Varessi led the way into the building and the lift, which took them up to the sixth floor and Flat 64. He rang the bell and when the door was opened, announced in peremptory tones who he was and the reason for his visit.

'I'm sorry,' said Stephanie, slowly and carefully, 'but could you say that again?'

'Señora,' said Alvarez in English, 'I have just arrived from Mallorca and would be grateful if you would answer some questions.'

'Mallorca?' She put her hand up to her face in an instinctive gesture of worry.

'May we come in?'

They entered. His immediate impression of her was that she was a warm woman; not young, not beautiful, and clearly not fashionable—her clothes were obviously chosen for comfort, not appearance—but the kind of woman a wise man hoped to marry, as opposed to the women he visualized in his more erotic moments.

She led the way through the small hall into the sitting/dining-room, which was dark and oppressive despite the sun outside, suggesting to Alvarez that the flat had been rented since he was convinced that she would have chosen furniture and furnishings much lighter in texture and colour. Through the large picture window there was a view over the town to the sea.

She came to a halt in the middle of the room. 'Are you here because Gerry's in some sort of trouble?'

Varessi, his expression bored, sat.

Alvarez did not answer her directly. 'When was the last time you saw him, señora?'

She shrugged her shoulders.

'Recently?'

'No.'

'Could you say approximately?'

'I suppose it must be about a year ago now. It was when Jacqueline . . .' She stopped. She then said sharply: 'What's happened to him?'

Her tone had not been anguished; more resentful. Then it seemed Oakley had been telling the truth about the state of their marriage. Alvarez was glad. News of his death might shock, but it would not tear her emotions apart. 'Señora, we have reason to think . . .' Briefly, he told her what had happened.

While he spoke, she had settled on the settee. Her expression remained composed, but the way in which she continually fiddled with one of the buttons on her frock suggested she was under considerable tension. When he'd finished speaking, there was a short pause, then she said: 'He fell overboard, even though the weather was fine?'

'It seems so.'

'Then he'd have had to watch the yacht sail on?'

He nodded.

'What a ghastly way to finish!'

He was not surprised that this thought horrified her—it had horrified him. One always hoped death would come quickly and unexpectedly . . . It already seemed clear that she would tell him nothing to confirm the possibility that Oakley had faked his death.

'I always used to think that he was someone who'd die in a way that would . . . To be thoroughly Irish, it would be larger than life. But then for years I saw him as larger than life. Jill, my sister, was always telling me I was a complete fool where he was concerned and I suppose she was right. I . . .' She stood, hurried from the room.

Varessi said: 'What the matter with her?'

'She's upset,' replied Alvarez shortly.

'Why?'

'I've just had to explain that her husband is dead.'

'But you told me they parted some time ago, so why's she in such a state?'

'It still comes as a shock.'

She returned, red-eyed, a few moments later. 'I'm sorry,' she said, as she sat.

'Señora, it is I who am sorry to have to bring such sad news.'

'It's not because I'm completely shattered—after all,

things hadn't gone right between us for a long time before we separated. But suddenly learning he's dead . . . If only things had been different . . . One day, Jill asked me point-blank if he was having an affair with Twinks. I was furious with her for daring to suggest such a thing. But a couple of weeks afterwards, I discovered he was. And Twinks was only one . . . I'm terribly old-fashioned when it comes to marriage. I've never believed one could go in for wife-swapping and that sort of thing and have any real marriage. Jill used to say I came straight out of the Ark. But in the end things went wrong for her and Bill and she were terribly unhappy.'

'When you left Bromley, señora, your marriage was already strained?'

'It was dead, only I just wouldn't admit it. I kept telling myself Gerry was merely fighting the seven-year itch and when he came to terms with getting older he'd stop chasing other women—but he didn't. We lived in Paris for a while and he was after women who were only half presentable, as if he was trying to make the city live up to its reputation. It was ridiculous and embarrassing, as well as painful.'

'What sort of work did he do while you were living in Paris?'

'I just don't know. That may sound silly, but it's true. In the beginning I tried to get him to talk about it, but he wouldn't. He was as secretive about that as he was over his women; only other people were eager to tell me about them.'

'Forgive my asking, but were there many affairs after you left Paris?'

'Enough to make me realize that all my hopes of becoming close again were so much moonshine. In the end, I suggested it was stupid to go on as we were and he agreed, with unflattering alacrity. That was the first time I acknowledged to myself that I no longer really meant anything to him.'

'And then?'

'He's always been very generous and he gave me more than enough money to lead the rather simple life I prefer.

We'd see each other occasionally. He'd ring and suggest we met and I'd tell myself it was meaningless, but each time I felt like a girl on her first heavy date because in spite of everything that had happened, I'd still wonder if he was going to say he'd become fed up with his rootless existence and how about trying to make a go of our lives together . . . He's never going to phone again, is he?'

'I'm afraid not, señora.'

'There were times when I longed to hear him say he wanted to come back and times when I never wanted to see or hear from him again. But now . . . I just don't know what I feel, except empty.'

'The last time you saw him, did he say anything at all about what he was doing?'

'Only that he'd just come from Mallorca. I knew he'd rented a house there, but I've never seen it.'

'Was he with you for long on that occasion?'

'Only one day. He'd come to give me some money . . . Your being here means that there was something wrong in what he was doing, doesn't it?'

'Unfortunately, yes.'

'What was it?'

'We think he was working with a man in England who was engaged in insider dealing.'

'Is that all? I was scared . . .' She stopped.

He said, very sadly: 'It is not all. There is also the possibility that in Mallorca he killed a man.'

She spoke with sudden fierceness. 'Don't be ridiculous.'

'The evidence . . .'

'You met him?'

'Yes.'

'Then you should know he couldn't ever do such a terrible thing.'

He wondered just how much a woman had to suffer before her faith in a man was finally destroyed and she could see him as he really was.

She'd noticed his expression. 'How can you begin to think he would?'

'He visited the house of the dead man on the afternoon of the murder and had a serious row; the murdered man had been swindling him and because of that the company he was running was in serious financial trouble . . .'

'I don't care. He couldn't do such a thing. He didn't dislike anyone that much. He looked at life with an amused irony so that nothing really shocked him—which I suppose is why he couldn't understand how his behaviour shocked me . . .' She became silent once more.

'Señora, do you know if he had a house or flat anywhere else besides the one in Mallorca?'

'Yes, he did.'

'Could you give me the address?'

'I could, but I won't.'

'Why not?'

'Because . . . Oh Christ!' She suddenly stood. 'I need a drink. What will you have?'

'Do you have a brandy, please?'

'And what about him?' She indicated Varessi.

After she'd served the drinks, she sat once more. 'Gerry used to say that drinking never really helped. He was wrong; it's helped me a lot . . . Does that shock you to hear?'

'Anything that eases pain is good. People who deny that have never known real pain.'

'You've known it, haven't you?'

He nodded.

'It's in your face. And that's why you're being so kind to me now. He—' she nodded at Varessi—'he'd never understand, not in a month of Sundays.'

'What's she saying?' demanded Varessi.

'That you remind her of one of the more adventurous racing drivers, but she can't remember his name,' replied Alvarez.

Varessi smiled complacently.

She finished her drink, looked at Alvarez, stood, went over to the cocktail cabinet and poured herself another. 'Why d'you want to know where Gerry had another house?'

'I'd like to go there and find out if there's anyone who's seen him recently.'

'No problem!' she said bitterly, as she returned to her chair. 'All you have to do is talk to Jacqueline Tabriz.'

It was the same christian name she had mentioned before. 'Is she a friend?'

'If you go in for euphemisms. She's his latest woman.'

'Have you met her?'

'No. If I had, I'd have . . . Oh God, would I? Would I have clawed her face, or would I have remained ladylike, as I was brought up to be no matter what the circumstances? Of course, in those days "the circumstances" did not include greeting one's husband's latest tart.'

'He told you about her?'

'Not a word. Give the devil his due, he never flaunted them in my face. I wouldn't know if that was out of respect for my feelings or for fear of what I'd do if I had definite proof.'

'Then how do you know about her?'

She drank.

'Please, señora, it is important.'

'Why?'

'Because I need to speak to her. Where does she live?'

There was a long silence. She drained her glass, then spoke, her voice now almost devoid of tone, as if she were being forced very reluctantly to recite in public. 'La Maison Rouge, Rue de Dunkerque, Nice. I thought how appropriate it was that his tart was living in a red house. I wonder if she's ever realized the significance? He'd have done immediately, of course, and had a chuckle. Do you want to know how I found out? They say that confession brings the peace of absolution; or the self-delusionment of the peace, which is just as useful. The last time he was here, the weather was very muggy and he was sweating heavily—he always did. He hated feeling tacky, so he had a shower. While he was in the shower-room, I had to go into my bedroom for something or other and his clothes were on the bed and his wallet had fallen out of his trouser pocket. Even as I picked it up, I thought of all those seaside postcards of wives going through their husbands' possessions . . . But I just couldn't stop myself seeing what was in it. There was a letter from her. I began reading it and then he came out of the shower-room so suddenly I didn't have time to do anything. I was so ashamed I wanted to sink through the floor, but as that remained solid, I started shouting like a fishwife. He just looked at me with that ironic smile which I knew so well and said there was another letter in his suitcase if I'd like to read that as well.

'As soon as he was dressed, he left. No further mention of the letter. Just a peck on the cheek and the hope that I'd managed to make lots of nice friends. I haven't. He understood me too well for my own good, but never seemed to realize that I gave him so much of myself that when he'd gone there wasn't much left, whereas he'd always withheld part of himself from me to have enough to offer others.' She picked up her glass, went to drink, found it was empty. 'And now I'll never see him again. So as he died, his last memory of me was probably of me shouting like a fishwife . . .'

'In time,' he said quietly, 'the memories will not hurt so much.'

'Perhaps. But they'll always hurt.'

He could not deny that. He stood. 'We'll go now. Thank you very much, señora.'

She looked up at him, then away. She did not speak again before they left, nor had she moved from the settee.

In the lift, Varessi said: 'What was she going on and on about?'

'Her husband had been betraying her.'

'Hardly surprising.'

Alvarez hoped that one day Varessi would discover that his wife had been as unfaithful to him as almost certainly he had been to her.

CHAPTER 22

Alvarez was a romantic, so he viewed Nice as he had always imagined it, not as it had become. He saw elegance where another would have seen only casual sloppiness, shops filled with quality, not discounts, restaurants where every single dish was a masterpiece, not fast food outlets . . .

'You did say Rue de Dunkerque?' asked the taxi-driver, talking around an unlit, sodden cigar.

'That's right.'

'I used to have a cousin who lived in the next street. Smarmy little sod went into politics and made a fortune.'

'Don't they all?'

'Not like here, they don't. Compared to the mob that runs this town, everyone else is a beginner. If I told you the half, you'd call me a liar.'

Were things really much worse here than they were anywhere else? Power meant money and money corrupted. But poverty corrupted just as much . . .

They turned a corner. 'Here we are. What was the number again?'

'The name's La Maison Rouge. I guess it's that place along on the right.'

They drew up alongside a house with very red brickwork and red shutters, obviously old, set in a large garden. Many years ago, Alvarez guessed, it had been built for a newly successful merchant, eager to underline his success. Since then, the area had clearly gone down in social standing, leaving the large house stranded.

He paid the fare, adding a generous tip, climbed out on

to the pavement, small suitcase in his left hand. The taxi drove away. Some children, playing an unusual form of hopscotch on the pavement looked at him for a while, then decided he was of little interest and returned to their game.

The wrought-iron gate was unlocked and he pushed it open and went through. The garden was almost totally overgrown and, perhaps as a result of seeing this neglect, he noticed that the house had broken coping stones, crumbling pointing, and flaking paint on many of the shutters.

Three stone steps led up to a small portico. He pressed the electric bell button to the right of the door, the top half of which was panelled with opaque red glass. He saw a form approach from inside, but could not tell whether it was male or female.

A woman opened the door. 'Gerry, I've been going crazy . . .' She stopped and stared at him with bitter disappointment.

'Mademoiselle Tabriz?'

'What do you want? Who are you?'

'My name is Inspector Alvarez, of the cuerpo general de policia; I'm from Mallorca.'

'Oh God, has something happened?'

Her appearance was provocative, initially suggesting that either it was a declaration of rebellion, or Stephanie's description of tart was an accurate one. The blouse was too tight and the neckline too plunging, making it clear she wore no brassière, the jeans hugged her thighs and buttocks, her make-up was garish and her hair was peroxide blonde. And yet he slowly gained the impression that under this crude exterior there was too much ability to care for the word 'tart' to be a true label—life quickly taught tarts that there was no room for weakness. She reminded him of someone, but whatever the point of resemblance was, it was too weak or shifting for him to be able to pin it down.

'Has something happened to Gerry?' she demanded, her voice high.

'May I come in?'

She moved to one side and he entered. If he were right, he thought sadly, and life had not sufficiently toughened her, she was going to be badly hurt.

The sitting-room was large, but gloomily dark because of the mimosa tree outside the window. On the heavy marble mantelpiece was a large photograph in an elaborate silver frame which showed her laughing gaily at Oakley, who was clowning with a woman's hat.

'For God's sake, tell me what's happened.'

He would have liked to put the facts so that she was left with some hope because then he would not be forced to witness her full misery, but because he knew that although there was no final proof, there was now no room for hope, he spoke bluntly. 'Mademoiselle, last Thursday night, Señor Oakley sailed out of Llueso Bay in a yacht. On Friday, when well out to sea, the yacht was boarded by members of the Spanish Navy and they found no one aboard.'

She stared at him, her face working. 'No! No,' she shouted. 'You're lying!'

'I'm afraid not.'

'He never sailed on it.'

'We know that he did and that he was aboard not long before the yacht was sighted. We can only presume that while he was eating something happened to take him up on deck—it may have been a boat-hook breaking loose and rolling about—and tragically he did not bother to wear the safety harness. He fell overboard.'

'If that had happened, he'd have swum back. He's a wonderful swimmer.'

'The self-steering gear was rigged so the yacht held its course.'

'But he can swim really fast.'

'I fear, not fast enough.'

She shivered; her face puckered; she began to whimper and then ran over to the enormous, clumsy settee and threw herself face downwards on to it and began to pound it with her feet.

At times like this, he hated his job; ten times fortunate the man who had to suffer only his own tragedies.

After a while, she became motionless; finally she twisted round and sat up.

'I am very sorry, but I have to ask you questions. When did you last hear from him?'

'He . . . he phoned.'

'What day was this?'

'Wednesday, Thursday; I don't know.'

'What did he say?'

'That he'd be back here in two days at the most. And ever since Saturday evening I've been waiting and getting more and more desperate . . . Please, isn't there a chance another boat could have picked him up?'

The harbour master had said that the odds were all against this having happened by a rescue craft having neither a radio to report the event nor making for the nearest port to land the survivor. Sadly, he shook his head.

She whimpered again, as if she had been hit.

She had been expecting Oakley at the latest on Saturday evening—this placed the phone call as having been made on the Thursday, which was when he had first heard that a detective had arrived from England.

'I've only known him for about a year,' she said, as if the unfairness of so brief a happiness might reverse the subsequent, tragic events. She went on, speaking in a distant voice, reliving the past: 'I was working in a pâtisserie and he came to buy bread. He was back the next day and the day after that and always he waited for me to serve him and the other girls began to joke about it. Adèle said he was too old for me, but she was just jealous. He asked me out on my day off and we went to a bistro that specialized in

Languedoc food and had a cassoulet. We laughed because
the waiter refused to understand his French and I had to
translate it . . .' She became silent.

'Did you know he was married?'

'He explained that his wife and he didn't get on well
together and so they lived apart. He didn't try to hide it
from me, if that's what you're thinking,' she said with
sudden anger.

'Mademoiselle, I am truly very sorry, but I must . . .'

She brushed aside his apologies. 'He'd always wanted to
live in the South, so he suggested we look for a house. I left
my job.'

'When did you come to Nice?'

'Last year, in November. It was cold and wet when we
started, but when we arrived here it was warm and sunny.
We rented this house while we looked for one to buy. It was
all so wonderful . . .

'We looked at lots of houses, but none of them was what
he wanted. And then, just before he went away the last time,
we found an old farmhouse near Iprey which was empty
and for sale and he said that that was exactly right. There
are hills and a view down the valley; and lots of vines. He
spoke to a local architect about all the alterations he'd want
doing. We walked round the land, planning the garden . . .
But now . . . But now we're never going to live there, are
we? And it was to be so lovely.'

She had lost a dream. But had it yet occurred to her that
she might have lost something more important in reality—
her security? 'Mademoiselle, do you have any money?'

'Of course I have.'

'Enough to keep yourself?'

'But Gerry gives me . . .'

Watching her face, he could judge how she suddenly
realized that Oakley's death was going to affect her far more
than just emotionally. Unless he had named her in his will,
she was now penniless. And would he have done such a

thing when she was no more than the last in a long line of women and he would have expected that line to lengthen?

'Don't you think you should make arrangements to return home as soon as possible?'

'I can't. When I left to come down here with Gerry, they said . . .'

'Whatever they said, it was only because they were hurt.'

'They were ashamed, but not on my account, on their own. They were afraid of what the neighbours would say. Oh God, in this day and age to worry about that!'

'Do you have enough money for the fare? If not, I'll give it to you.'

Her expression changed abruptly. 'Oh God, I wish there were more people like you in the world.'

The vehemence with which she'd spoken surprised him. Had she divined what kind of a man Oakley really was, but had been fighting to ignore that knowledge?

Salas said sarcastically: 'Then is that proof enough, even for you?'

'Yes, señor,' replied Alvarez.

'You're not going to tell me in two days' time that he isn't dead, he's alive and well and living in Outer Mongolia?'

'Unfortunately, it is now quite certain that he drowned.'

'Unfortunately? It saves us a great deal of trouble.'

'I was thinking of all the emotional distress that his death has caused.'

'Our job is concerned with facts, not emotions. Inform England, then make out your report and see it's on my desk by tomorrow morning.'

'But, señor, that's impossible in so complicated a matter as this.'

'And whose damned fault is it that it's been so complicated?'

CHAPTER 23

The heat, considering it was now the middle of September, was exceptional. Tourists sweated on the beaches, which were littered with empty bottles of sun-tan lotion, and doctors treated so many cases of sunburn that their minds became filled with thoughts of the extra winter holidays they could now afford . . .

Braddon, waiting in a corridor in the justice building, was called into court.

The room was small, rectangular, and except for the two doorways and single small window, lined with filing cabinets and cupboards. The court official, a man in his late twenties, sat at a desk and typed the statements as they were made; both his desk and a second one nearer the window were piled so high with papers and files that to someone not versed in the mysteries of the law they appeared to be in inextricable confusion. The two doorways were directly opposite each other and between them passed a stream of people, some of whom murmured brief apologies for the disturbances they caused. The four lawyers—representing the three defendants and Braddon—stood in a rough semi-circle around the desk at which the official typed.

The official looked up and spoke to Braddon. 'Please be seated, señor.'

Braddon, who understood just enough Spanish to realize what had been said, sat. Butterflies were stamping about in his stomach and making him feel sick. He remembered trials whose whole course had been altered by the brilliance of counsel—Birkett, cross-examining with quiet but devastating effect—or the stupidity of the accused—Wilde, too concerned with being clever. Letitia had said: 'Just tell the truth.' But jesting Pilate had asked what was truth and had not stayed for the answer, knowing that there could not be one that would always be true.

The official, speaking rapidly, addressed Braddon. This time, Braddon understood nothing. His lawyer leaned forward. 'Say yes.'

He said yes.

The lawyer for the architect raised a sheet of paper, read, looked at Braddon over the top of it and spoke.

'Say no,' said Braddon's lawyer.

He said no.

There were three more questions, to each of which he was advised to say no.

The lawyer for the aparejador consulted his file, looked up, asked a question of much greater length.

'Say yes,' said Braddon's lawyer.

He said yes.

There were three more yeses and two more noes.

The lawyer for the builder spoke at inordinate length.

'Say you don't know,' said Braddon's lawyer.

He said he didn't know, four times.

The official pulled out a sheet of paper from the typewriter and put it down on several others. He spoke to Braddon.

'Sign,' said Braddon's lawyer.

He signed.

The lawyers and Braddon filed out of the courtroom into the corridor, the lawyers for the architect and the aparejador laughing over something highly amusing.

'You want to eat some coffee?' asked Braddon's lawyer, a pleasant man whose English was not quite as fluent as he believed.

They left the building and went down the street to a bar where they ordered two coffees. If it had been slightly later, Braddon would have asked for a brandy. He had tensed himself for a trial and a whiplash duel with eagle-eyed counsel, but instead there had merely been some further form of preliminary hearing, the nature of which entirely escaped him.

His lawyer drank quickly. 'Now, I leave; much work to make. Thank you for coffee. Goodbye, sweet dreams.'

'Here, hang on a minute.'

'Yes, you want to ask?'

'When's something going to happen?' The familiar, angry sense of frustration gripped his mind. 'Why can't you get them to understand that it's urgent? The bloody cracks are getting worse all the time and if something isn't done soon, the whole house will fall down.'

'I do not comprehend.'

'I'm saying that I want to know when the trial's going to be.'

His lawyer looked curiously at him. 'That was trial. Now, I come.' He started to walk away.

'But . . . but there wasn't any judge.'

He came to a stop. 'No judge in such court.'

'That . . . that's impossible.'

'Very possible; is always.'

A trial without a judge? Braddon wondered if that morning he'd inadvertently walked through a looking-glass. 'How can you have a verdict without a judge?'

'No verdict.'

A sense of panic caused him to shout: 'I'll contact the British Ambassador.'

'No verdict until judge reads papers and decides. We win.'

He slowly calmed down as he realized that the procedure was not as anarchic as he had first believed. 'Then when will he read the papers and decide and give his verdict? This afternoon?'

His lawyer thought that so funny that he laughed until be began to choke.

*

Alvarez had spent much of the day in a village not far from Andratx and on his return journey he chose to take the old road rather than the autoroute. Just past a restaurant, advertised by a mule carriage which stood on a concrete plinth, he saw a large billboard proclaiming that the country's finest development, La Portaña, lay a kilometre to the right. On impulse, he decided to turn off and visit the urbanización.

It was obvious that the tempo of work had picked up sharply from when he'd last been there. The two apartment blocks were once more under active construction, there was activity on several new plots, the grass in the square had just been cut and two men were working in the flowerbeds, sprinklers were on, and a lorry with a lifting hoist was lowering a mature palm into a hole. Vidal had correctly foretold the course of events, he thought. The banks had taken possession, had resold to the waiting predator, and this other property company was now all set to make a large profit. Curious to know whether Vich had been made redundant, as feared, he parked outside the wooden hut that was the office and went in. He recognized the typist, but not the young man who came up to the counter and spoke to him. He asked if Vich was still working there.

Vich shook hands with considerable energy, then led the way into his small, inner office.

'I was passing by,' said Alvarez, 'so came to see how things were. More than once, I've wondered whether you survived the new ownership.'

'No new owner and I'm still here. And, what's more, Andreu y Soler are looking at another possible development so things are very much more cheerful.'

'Don't say the banks relented at the last moment—that sounds very untypical.'

'They extended the time limit because a German company showed a great deal of interest in injecting the necessary capital into Andreu y Soler.'

'Good for them! Who found them?'

'I don't know for sure, because I'm not in that side of finance, but the word is that it was Señor Oakley, just before his unfortunate death. That man must have had a tongue of gold.'

'And presumably the German company finally did invest?'

'They certainly did. And that was the end of our money problems.'

'Have things changed much?'

'Not really. There was a lot of talk that the only way of making certain the development really prospered was to reduce prices and aim for a more popular, and therefore wider, market, but instead the reverse happened; prices were upped and the German market was targeted. And it worked! Land went up to twelve thousand a square metre and the houses had to cost a minimum of sixty million. Explain that to an Englishman or a Frenchman and he either has a fit or laughs. But the Germans, with their currency up in the stratosphere, become more and more interested. The ratio of contracts to inquiries is rising all the time.'

'What was the date when the banks gave their extension?'

'The middle of July.'

'And when did the German company make its decision?'

'I heard about it at the end of the month, when I'd given up all hope of keeping the job and was wondering what was the kindest way of cutting my throat.'

'So presumably they hadn't finally made up their minds until about then?'

'Knowing the situation vis-à-vis the banks, they can't have done.'

Then how, wondered Alvarez, had the company been persuaded to invest in Andreu y Soler when Oakley, the man who'd introduced them to the proposition, had just died in circumstances that suggested he was far from the

honest businessman they must have believed, and would
have demanded, they were dealing with? . . . And suddenly
he identified the likeness he had seen weeks previously in
Jacqueline Tabriz's face.

Alvarez's mind was so perturbed that when he returned to
Llueso he did not drive straight home and pour himself the
first of several strong drinks, but instead parked close to the
guardia post, went up to his office, and slumped down in
the chair behind the desk and stared at the opened, but
shuttered, window.

After a time, he roused himself and used the phone to
find out the telephone number of the Nice police. He dialled
that and spoke to a woman who referred him to a sergeant,
who had the call transferred to an inspector. The inspector,
rather grumpily, agreed to do as asked.

Nice called back at seven-fifteen.

'We've spoken to the estate agents. The house was let on
the fourteenth of July. The tenant was a young widow,
whose husband had just died, by the name of Madame
Brinaud. She took it for six months and paid the rent in full
in advance.'

'Did she have to present papers to be granted a lease?'

'Indeed.'

'Is she still living there?'

'One of our chaps went with someone from the estate
agents along to La Maison Rouge. It was empty and there
are none of her belongings around. It certainly looks as if
she's left.'

'Without any word to the agents?'

'None; but as they say, since the rent's paid for several
months to come, there was no call for her to contact them.
Perhaps she intends to return soon.'

'I rather doubt it.'

CHAPTER 24

On Wednesday morning, Alvarez sat at his desk and stared through the opened and unshuttered window at the sun-blasted wall of the house on the opposite side of the street. He heard a woman begin to sing; a car hooted; young boys shouted obscenities with all the pleasure of new discoveries. Did he speak to Salas now? Not yet, he immediately decided. Not while there was still room for his being wrong. After all, there might be a reasonable explanation of why Madame Brinaud had also called herself Mademoiselle Tabriz; why she had told him she had moved into the house the previous November, when in fact it had been this July . . .

He telephoned the site office at La Portaña and spoke to Vich. He asked for the name and address of the German company which had invested money in Andreu y Soler. After trying, and failing, to learn why the request was being made, Vich gave this to him.

He dialled the Munich number. A woman answered the call and failed to understand his Spanish, English, French, or even the few words he thought he knew in German. Then a man came on the line who spoke almost faultless English.

'You are the Spanish police and want to speak about something in connection with an investment we've made in the Spanish firm of Andreu y Soler? What is the matter?' There was a note of concern in his voice.

A firm of highly conservative rectitude, he thought, which would recoil from the first whiff of scandal. 'There's nothing wrong, señor. I just thought you might be able to help me by saying how I can get in touch with Señor Oakley.' This was the moment of truth. Would a short silence be followed by angry surprise? Get hold of a man who'd drowned back in July? What the hell sort of a policeman was he . . .?

'Why are you ringing us to find this out?'

'Andreu y Soler suggested you as being the most likely people to know. He is not at the address they have and the matter is urgent.'

'Do you mind telling me roughly why you wish to speak to him?'

'He's a potential witness in a case and I have to verify certain facts as soon as I can.'

'Would you hold on a moment, please.'

As he waited, his thoughts raced ahead . . .

'Hullo. We have a Swiss number where he can be contacted. Would you like me to give you that?'

He wrote the number down and thanked them. He telephoned the Swiss number.

A voice said in French, then German: 'This is an answering machine. At the moment, Gerald Oakley is away, but if you will leave a message he will receive it very shortly. Please speak after the last of the four pips. You have sixty seconds in which to leave your message.'

The pips sounded.

'This is Inspector Alvarez, from Llueso. Today is the seventeenth of September, fifty-four days after you drowned in the sea, many miles off Mallorca. Will you please telephone me at my office.' He gave the number, then cut the connection. It occurred to him that anyone—other than Oakley—who had heard him, would place him as either crazy or drunk.

He slumped back in the chair. But for one thing, Oakley could have disappeared and the rest of the world would always have believed him dead. Ironically, that one thing was his pride which demanded that he prove his honesty.

He was a man of many contradictions; happy to benefit

from illegal activities, yet demanding of himself the highest standards of honesty in all dealings with his dishonest partner; clever and hard-headed, yet naïvely trusting when it came to the people he chose to work for him . . .

Roig had swindled Andreu y Soler and put the whole urbanización at risk. Another man might well have shrugged his shoulders and told his partner that it was just bad luck —money earned by swindling had been lost to a swindler —but because Oakley had a total sense of loyalty and honesty, because he felt guilty for not having detected what was happening soon enough, he'd desperately sought to find a way of saving everything. And it seemed he might have succeeded when disaster struck—Roig had been murdered. He didn't need to be half as clever as he was to appreciate how likely he was to be named the main suspect. And let it be known that he was suspected of murder and any firm, let alone one as conservatively honest as the German one, would withdraw. So he had had to do something to keep the police at bay either until they found out who the real murderer was or until he could gain enough time for the German company to reach a decision and to invest their money and so reach the point of no return . . .

How to keep the police at bay for long enough? He must have reached the answer at least in part due to his sense of ironic humour. Wrong-foot them, again and again, until they were reluctant openly to accuse him, let alone arrest him, until quite certain they had all the facts, exactly, precisely, and incontrovertibly . . . Since he was apparently involved in the murder, first make it appear he had fled the island in an attempt to escape. Then, when he was being sought as the killer, let the evidence suggest that far from having killed, he had been killed. When his murderer was being sought, return to life and explain away all those details which had pointed to his death. Finally, when enough time had been gained, 'die' once more . . .

He'd learned from the note Beatriz had left that an
Englishman had arrived who clearly was working with the
Spanish police. Obviously, a detective come to question him
about the insider dealings in London and Ashley Developments. With no way of judging how much the English police
now knew, or how close to arrest and subsequent deportation
he was, he'd realized that he had to disappear at once. But
although the German company were very interested, they
had not yet finally committed themselves. Now there was
only one way of winning through. A faked suicide. But at
such a time this was going to be viewed with the deepest
possible suspicion, however brilliantly staged. So the question became, what sort of proof would overcome even that
degree of suspicion? And the answer had been, proof provided by people who appeared emotionally to have the most
reason for wishing him alive . . .

The setting sun was still visible above the mountains, but
the burning heat had gone from it; animals moved from the
shade they'd used all day, villagers carried chairs out into
the streets and gossiped.

The telephone in Alvarez's office rang and he answered
the call.

'Good evening, Inspector, it's Gerald Oakley here. I
confess I had hoped I wouldn't receive your call, but there
was always something about you which warned me that I
might; and if I refer to a suggestion of dogged persistence,
please accept that as a compliment and in no way condescending or critical. Now, before we go any further, satisfy
my curiosity on one point. Why leave a message which gives
me due warning that although I may have fooled all the
world some of the time, unfortunately I've only managed to
fool some of the world all the time. Surely you should have
remained silent and travelled to Switzerland and asked the
Swiss police to arrest me on a charge of murder before I
realized my danger?'

'There were really two reasons, señor.'

'Which were?'

'First, I was sure I would not succeed.'

'Why not?'

'I was certain you had foreseen the possibility and therefore must have worked out how to circumvent the danger.'

'You have a flattering faith in my abilities.'

'With reason. After all, I had discovered how you had foreseen the possibility that you would be investigated too closely for your own safety and therefore at some stage it might be necessary to "die" in an accident; and that the only way in which such a "death" would be accepted would be on the evidence of someone who must be presumed to want you very much alive. And the way in which you set about that was to erase the address of your wife in Italy on your passport, knowing that a forensic laboratory could eventually raise it. If an attempt is apparently made to hide something, the overwhelming inference has to be that the reason this was done was in order to conceal it—not to reveal it—and therefore whatever was hidden will be accepted as genuine. So who would doubt that your wife had been living in San Remo for as long as she claimed, or would question her distress and natural hatred for her late husband's final mistress, whose address in Nice she just happened to have . . .?

'When a man can plan ahead like that, he is not going to leave himself wide open to disaster through a simple matter like providing a third party with a telephone number which can easily be traced. I imagine that you have an accommodation address which you never go near, but in which you have installed an answering machine capable of being activated by remote control. This enables you not only to keep in touch with your business interests, but also to learn about dangers without ever placing yourself in jeopardy.'

'I have to award you full marks for perspicacity,

Inspector . . . Let's move on. What was the second reason?'

'You did not murder Roig.'

'I'm gratified you've accepted that fact, but also surprised. When I had the pleasure of meeting you, you left me in little doubt that I was suspect number one.'

'Since then I have learned that you are a man of honour.'

'As Brutus would tell you, an honourable man can kill.'

'Certainly, but only in a moment of overwhelming passion when he has not planned and does not really know what he's doing. The murderer went into the kitchen—quite a distance away—to get the knife and returned to the sitting-room to stab Roig, which means he knew exactly what he was doing; he stabbed him more than once and with brutal force, which either suggests a frenzy or a deliberate intention to kill, and because he had gone to the kitchen for the knife he was not in a frenzy.'

'My respect for you increases all the time . . . If you don't believe I murdered Roig, exactly why have you phoned me?'

'To ask you some questions.'

'Can there be any left?'

'Have you and your wife separated, señor?'

'And what is the relevance of that?'

'Because . . .'

'Because what?'

'I hope it is not true and that Señora Oakley told me that merely as part of the story that was designed to lead me on to the woman who appeared to be your mistress.'

'The best way of answering you is to get someone else to do it. Hang on a moment.'

A woman said: 'Inspector, rest assured that if I suspected for one second that my husband had a mistress, I'd deal with her in no uncertain manner.'

'I'm so glad.'

'What a nice man you are! Sue's absolutely right.'

'Is Sue your daughter who was calling herself both Jacqueline Tabriz and Madame Brinaud? And who was trained in acting in England?'

'Quite correct.'

'She is a very good actress, just as you are.'

'Thank you. I think you should know that she is feeling very contrite. You were so nice, she hated deceiving you and when you offered to pay her fare back home, she could hardly refrain from confessing everything.'

He ceased to feel embarrassed at the way in which he had been so thoroughly hoodwinked. 'Señora, may I ask a very personal question? Right at the end of my visit to your daughter, she seemed very, very bitter and I cannot believe that that was a false emotion. Has she been unhappy recently?'

'You are much too discerning. Yes, she's been exceedingly unhappy, but things are gradually getting better. She went with a touring company to France, where she was educated, and met Michel Brinaud, fell in love with him, brought him home for us to meet, and said she was thinking of marrying him. Gerry, who's a sharp judge of character, said he was a rotter. Couldn't have been less tactful, but then there are times when he acts like a bull in a china shop. Naturally, she went off and married the wretched man. She suffered eighteen months of hell and then cleared out.'

'I do hope she soon finds someone nice.'

'I'll pass on your wishes—she'll really appreciate them ... Now, would you like another word with Gerry?'

'If I may, please.'

Oakley came back on the line.

'Señor, can you tell me anything about the murder of Roig?'

'Nothing.'

'What really happened the day he was murdered?'

'I've always told you the truth except in one detail; I drove away much later than I admitted. Which of course was a silly mistake, since it pinned me down as a liar.'

'And were you arguing with him all the time?'

'Arguing, pleading, threatening, promising, doing everything I could think of to try and make him repay the money, or at least a sufficient part of it to keep the bank sharks at bay. In the end, by which time he was half tight, I accepted that he wasn't going to repay a peseta whatever I said— either because he wouldn't or couldn't, having, as he claimed, gambled the whole lot away.'

'Did you see anyone near the house when you left?'

'No.'

'Was there much other traffic?'

'If you mean on the dirt track, none at all.'

'And on the road close to the dirt track?'

'A couple of cars, no more.'

'Did you notice a motorized bike of any sort?'

'I don't think so.'

'Then I have no more questions.'

'No? You surprise me. Don't you want to know if I am working hand-in-glove with the insider dealer in London?'

'I haven't the slightest doubt that you are.'

Oakley chuckled.

CHAPTER 25

For once, Dolores was not working in the kitchen; she was on her own, watching the television. Alvarez poured himself a generous brandy, settled in one of the chairs. The programme came to an end and she used the remote control to switch the set off.

'Where's everyone?' he asked.

'Jaime's gone to see Bertine and the children are playing with Angel . . . You're home early.'

'I've been feeling very tired.'

'If you drank less, you'd feel more wide awake.'

'I'm tired because I've been working too hard . . . Dolores, if a young woman's been having an affair with an older man and is now in trouble and ought to go home to her family, but won't, saying she can't, what would you think is the real reason?'

She swung round, spoke in a shocked voice. 'Enrique!'

'Here, you're not thinking it's me, are you? . . . You women have one-track minds.'

'That's half a track more than you men.'

He drank, rested the glass on the arm of the chair. 'You'd think she was pregnant, wouldn't you?'

'Of course.'

'Funny! It just never occurred to me at the time.'

'Then it is you!'

'No, it damn well is not!'

'You are quite certain?'

'I've never so much as run my hands up under her skirt.'

'There's no need to be vulgar,' she said severely.

The owner of the house in Camino S'on Perragut said that Vidal was in his room. Alvarez went through to the patio and then up the wooden stairs to the bedroom, which vibrated to the noise of the record-player.

'Turn it off,' he shouted.

Vidal, showing none of the contemptuous courtesy he had before, hesitated, then, his expression sullen, leaned over the bed and switched off the player. Alvarez crossed to the chair, removed some clothes that were on it, and sat.

'Whatever it is you want, you'd better hurry. I'm due at work soon,' Vidal said.

'Work can wait.'

'Why d'you keep chasing me?'

'Because I need to confirm the reason why you murdered Roig.'

'Here . . . That's not bloody funny.'

'Señorita Garcia is pregnant, isn't she?'

'Why ask me?'

'With her father dead and no closer male relative, you're head of the family, aren't you, and therefore its honour lies in your hands? Down your way, you're great people for family honour.'

'We've a sight more of it than you have on this island.'

'True. These days, we have far too little; but is that more reprehensible than having too much? . . . Do you remember telling me about mujeriegos and how they had to be dealt with brutally in order to restore a family's honour; but you'd never treat Roig as one because no one in the family, either in Bodón or Posuna, would ever learn about your cousin's affair? But when you'd discovered she was pregnant, you knew that no longer could anything be hidden; the family must learn the truth and when they did they'd be disgraced unless you, as was your duty, acted.'

'You don't understand.'

'I understand. What I don't do, is sympathize.'

'Then you don't understand.'

'All right, have it your way and now make me understand. Tell me how it was. When you went there on the Monday night, what were you intending to do?'

'I didn't go . . .' Vidal said loudly, then stopped as he saw the expression on Alvarez's face.

'I know you went there. I've found someone who saw you on your Vespa,' Alvarez bluffed.

There was a long silence. Eventually, Vidal said in a low, strained voice: 'I wanted to make him agree to divorce his wife and marry Eulalia.'

'How did he react to the suggestion?'

'First, he was surprised, then he laughed.'

'Which shows what a very stupid man he was when it came to human relationships. One should never laugh at a man of real honour, should one?'

'Stop sneering or I'll . . .'

'Stick a knife into me as you stuck one into him?'

Vidal's expression crumpled. 'I didn't mean to.'

'The cry of every murderer after he's caught.'

'I swear I didn't.'

'The knife just slipped as you went to castrate him and thereby regain your family's honour?'

'I . . . I . . .'

'Well?'

'I wasn't going to.'

'Going to what?'

'Castrate him?'

'Why not? You'd named him mujeriego.'

'Can't you see?'

'Probably. But you're going to tell me.'

'I . . . I couldn't do it.'

'You couldn't act like a man of honour?'

His shame was obvious.

'So what did you do?'

'I threatened him. I told him what would happen to him if he lived in Bodón. But he realized I . . . I couldn't actually do it. He began to jeer at me. He said I was all bluster. And then he said he was going to throw me out and started coming at me.'

'And you were scared?'

'I wasn't scared, but . . . I pulled my knife. He went to knock it out of my hand and slipped and . . . Oh God, it slid into his guts and he clawed at it and then collapsed on to the chair . . .' He covered his face with his hands.

'Very dramatic, but all a lie.'

'I tell you, it's what happened.'

'The truth is, you went into the kitchen and chose a knife, knowing exactly what you were going to do and that was to murder with malice aforethought.'

'I didn't go near the kitchen. I don't even know where it is.'

Alvarez visualized the route from the sitting-room to the kitchen which involved going down two fairly long passages; a route that could never be called obvious. 'You talked about "pulling your knife—" were you carrying one on you?'

'In my village, every man does because . . .'

'The less I know about your village, the better. Describe your knife.'

It in no way resembled the kitchen knife found in Roig's body.

Julia was picking peppers; both large, cone-shaped ones which had turned a bright red and also very much smaller ones, thin and elongated, that were a dusky red and which contained the fires of hell.

'Have you time for a word?' Alvarez asked.

She straightened up slowly and reached round to the small of her back and pressed down with clenched fist to ease the pain.

He picked up the two cane baskets and carried them to the patio, where he sat while she went into the house. She returned with two glasses and an earthenware jug of wine which she put down on the rough wooden table. He filled the two glasses and passed her one. 'I've learned several things since I last saw you.' He drank. 'The señorita is pregnant, isn't she?'

'Poor girl.'

'Why does she not have an abortion?'

'Because her religion forbids it, of course.'

Had it not also forbidden her fornication? 'Will she have the baby adopted here, on the island?'

'I don't know.'

'But she'll never dare return to her village with it?'

'Of course not. There, women don't flaunt their little bastards for all the world to see their shame.'

'So what's going to happen to her?'

'How should I know?' she said tiredly. 'Perhaps Carlos will marry her.'

'In spite of all that's happened and the fact that he's her cousin?'

'A distant enough cousin. And I've seen him look at her with desire.'

'Is she fond of him?'

'When a woman's with another man's child and no sight of marriage to him, how can she afford to worry about love?'

'Was it to save Vidal that you pulled out the knife that was in the body and which you recognized as his and replaced it with a kitchen knife?'

She spoke scornfully. 'Of course not.'

'Then it was to try and save the señorita's reputation?'

She nodded.

He'd correctly deduced Oakley's innocence, but on a totally false premise; he thought Oakley would appreciate the irony of that.

She spoke stolidly, as if the answer was of small moment. 'Will I have to go to prison?'

'That's up to the courts, not me.'

'If I do, who'll look after Adolfo?'

'It would do him good to have to look after himself.'

She shook her head as she pushed the jug across the table. 'Fill up. There's more inside if that's not enough.'

When he returned to the office, he was finally going to have to nerve himself up to telephoning Salas to say that, yet again, Oakley had returned to life. So the longer his return could be delayed, the better. He refilled his glass to the brim.